Cornelius Montegue
Unlicensed Junior Private Investigator
The Case of the Displaced Art Class

# Cornelius Montegue
## Unlicensed Junior Private Investigator
### The Case of the Displaced Art Class

Michael Maurice Franchetti

Cover Art By: Christina M. Young

**Publishing History**
First E-book Edition: April, 2022
First Paperback Edition: April, 2022
First Hardback Edition: April, 2022

Book Design By: Michael Maurice Franchetti
Cover Art By: Christina M. Young

ISBN: 979-8-9857069-1-8 (E-Book)
ISBN: 979-8-9857069-2-5 (Paperback)
ISBN: 979-8-9857069-3-2 (Hardback)

Published By
Michael Maurice Franchetti
www.MichaelMauriceFranchetti.com

Dedicated to all of those who believed in me and are no longer with us. I am sorry I could not finish in time for you to enjoy it.

# Contents

# Emergency Shutdown

Montegue Investigations was a Private Investigation Agency. Cornelius Montegue and his wife Olivia Montegue were the Named Partners. Michelangelo Durelly was their silent and equal partner. Jenna Arton was their newest junior partner. Each of them brought something to the agency. They usually worked on multiple cases at one time. However, this case was the biggest one of the agency's short but rising notoriety. It required all hands-on deck, and they have only seen each other sparingly during the ordeal. They were also relying on one particular receptionist from the temp agency and were certain they were going to offer her a full-time position, however, because of the complexity of what was going on, Cornelius asked her to take the rest of the month off. Unfortunately, not only did she take him up on the offer, but she also resigned, effective immediately. Therefore, everyone was taking on extra duties.

Jenna Arton had been working non-stop for the last three weeks, with barely a break. For the last thirty-six hours, she had been working on the case non-stop, until she got a call from Olivia less than an hour ago. Olivia was asking for some information on the case when suddenly, a commotion happened on her end of the line, she could hear her phone hit the ground and bounce, Cornelius shouted watch out, Olivia scream in pain, a couple of shots, and finally, the phone went silent. Jenna went into panic mode and tried to get her back. She did not hesitate, after failing to get her back on the phone before calling Cornelius. He did not answer as well, and her mind was racing with a thousand possibilities of what could have happened. Suddenly, her anxiety kicked in, causing her to panic as the room began to spin. However, just before she blacked out, she noticed the picture of Cornelius and Olivia's wedding. She locked eyes on it, smiled, then looked for another picture, and continued to focus on the good memories associated with them until she regained control of her anxiety. Her window was small to contain her anxiety before it became a full anxiety attack, so she sat down at the receptionist's desk to prepare for her counter measures, however she did not know how she got there. Disregarding her relocation to the receptionist's desk, she took a deep breath, counted to thirty, then fifty, and finally to seventy-seven before completely gaining control again. She took several deep breaths as regained control, took a drink of her now cold coffee, and called both Cornelius and Olivia. Frustrated with her failure, her mind scrambled for a solution and remembered to herself, 'Michelangelo!' She called him immediately.

"Hello," he responded as he answered the phone. The warmth of his voice filled her with hope as she savored it for a couple of microseconds before telling him what happened. "Relax, I am on my way to their last known location," he replied as the sound of his car's tires squealed. She could hear him shift before he continued, "I will be in touch!" Suddenly, the phone went silent after he hung up.

She sighed in relief as she focused on what she was working on before the call. However, between her lack of sleep and her near full anxiety attack, she passed out on the receptionist's desk, and her long blonde hair sprawled out over her keyboard and engulfing her hands, which she was using as pillows. Her nap on top of the desk was extremely overdue and slept for what she thought was an eternity. However, it was slightly less than an hour before her phone began vibrating on the desk, and she shifted in her sleep. It was going off repeatedly, cutting off just before it would go to voicemail, and then starting up again. It was slowly vibrating across the desk as if it were trying to escape the desk to the floor below. After the fifth or sixth attempts of getting through to her, she shifted to free up her right hand, then crept it toward the phone until her hand emerged from her hair. Her hand shuffled along the desk, blindly looking for the phone, as if it had a life of its own. Her chipped and unmaintained black nail polish tried to glisten under the lights as her hand moved across the desk. Finally, she bumped it, stopped instantly as to not knock it on the floor, raised her hand, then set it down on the phone. Wrapping her fingers around the phone, she grasped it, and pulled it back into the mass of sprawled hair upon the desk. This was her personal phone, and she answered with not quite awake tone in her voice, "Who is (cleared her throat and smacked her lips) this?"

"Hey Jenna. It's Cornelius," responded the voice on the other end of the line.

She excitedly sat up, put the phone on the receptionist's desk, and placed it on speaker. She started pulling her blond hair back, interlaced the two braids on either side of her head, and worked them into a ponytail, and asked, "What is going on? How are the two of you? Do you know how scared I was? Is Olivia alright?"

Suddenly, her hazel eyes flashed wide, and her world paused in time for a moment as he responded, "I do not know. Olivia was in bad shape, but I left her with Pierre and Michelangelo."

He was silent after that until she snapped out of it and asked, "How bad?"

"Sorry, but I need you to focus and carry out my instructions to the letter," he responded coldly.

She could tell from the sound in his voice how bad the situation is, she took a deep breath and asked, "What do you need me to do?" He recited a set of several instructions.

He could hear in her voice she had more questions. However, before she could ask them, he added, "Before you ask anything else, you do not have a lot of time, and I need you to carry out the instructions I gave you."

"Ok," she responded as he hung up.

She gathered her stuff, walked down the hall, and entered the server room. Pulling the keyboard down for the command terminal, which also turned it on, she waited for the screen to finish booting up and ask her to enter the main key code. Once she did, the screen flashed, and another screen came up waiting for more commands. Without hesitation she started entering the codes in the order Cornelius had texted her. The screen stated it was waiting for confirmation, and a list of all ten interfaces appeared. Each interface labeled with the typical Cornelius precision. First were their four phones, Cornelius, Olivia's, and Michelangelo's confirmed as in standby, but hers was showing active. Cornelius told her to do her phone last. So, she would not lose the codes for the six terminals and the last six interfaces on the screen. She scurried back to her office, typed in Cornelius' name, followed by hers, and the numbers zero and four. The screen confirmed the code and asked are you sure. She hit yes and waited for it to say standby. Once complete, she went around the office and typed in the remainder of the codes in their appropriate terminals. All the codes started with Cornelius and then the name of the operator, except for the receptionist desk, which was 'receptionist', followed by the two-digit code of when they joined the agency. She proceeded in the following order: the receptionist's desk, Olivia's, Cornelius', the law library, and then finally to Michelangelo's. She entered the server room again, and noticed all terminals registered as standby, and she entered the code into her phone.

Suddenly, her phone flashed standby for only a second, until they switched to confirmed. A screen popped up on the monitor asking, "Are you sure?" She clicked yes, and they all switched from confirmed to pending as another pop-up window asked, "Do you have the final code?" She smiled because this was the easy one to remember, as she typed, "Cornelius and Olivia Montegue." After she entered the final code, it asked her to confirm, and she did. Immediately afterword her phone shut off and an icon stating it was transferring occupied the entire screen. Watching the main screen of the command terminal as all the interfaces confirmed they transferred. Once they were all done, the transferred notification turned to purged, and each interface showed its progression of the purge status one by one.

As the last one completed, the command terminal's screen flashed, and two lines came up under the heading server transfer in progress. The top line was overall completion, and the second line was the individual server's completion. After each one completed, it would start the next automatically. The screen flashed after the transfer completed, and the screen popped up a similar screen as the last. However, instead of transferring it said purging. A couple of seconds later, it finished, the screen went blank, the servers no longer flashed any lights, and the office got quieter.

She did not know where the information was going and did not care. Cornelius would never tell her so she could maintain plausible deniability. After she purged everything, she pulled another phone out of her purse and pressed the speed dial number one, added the six-digit code she knew by heart and waited for the call to connect. A few seconds later, Cornelius answered, "I noticed the transfer started. Now, before you go to Olivia, I need you to do one more thing for me."

"Absolutely," she responded as she listened to his instructions before he hung up. She went to the law library and started looking through the books and binders for the one he instructed her to find. Once she found the correct binder, she smiled with confidence, and she put it into her backpack next to her laptop. This was her personal laptop, which was never part of the Montegue Investigations network. Using the second phone to summon an Uber, she exited the office, locked the office door behind her, walked down the hall, and entered the elevator.

On her way down in the elevator, Michelangelo texted with the hospital room number. She pulled her phone out to confirm the text, smiled, and put it back into her pocket as the elevator came to a stop. She exited the elevator and then the building just as the Uber pulled up, as if she timed it that way. Walking up to the Uber, she opened the door, confirmed the driver matched the picture in the app, and got in.

As they drove away, her phone rang, and she answered, "Hello."

"Hey Jenna, this is Cleopatra Montegue. Cornelius gave me this number in case of emergencies. I am looking for Cornelius and I know you will not help me find him. I am sure you understand we need him for questioning about Olivia, and I am also sure you know is on the run.

Please, if he contacts you, have him call me. I would like to handle this before I have to as the Chief of Detectives."

"If he calls, I will do what I can," Jenna replied before hanging up.

As the Uber driver skillfully moved through town, Jenna's thoughts of Olivia's fate overwhelmed her, and she stared absentmindedly out the window. Finally, they made a turn, which confirmed she knew where they were, and she got ready to get out of the car. The Uber driver pulled up the car in front of the hospital's emergency room entrance. She took a deep breath and stepped out of the car. As she approached the doors of the hospital, they automatically opened. Stepping through the doorway, she continued until she made her way to the information desk. People in the lobby looked at Jenna as she walked by, with either admiration for or contempt for either her personal style or her authentic beauty. A couple of husbands got an elbow as she passed from their spouses. Her clothes did not command respect: Jeggings, Avril Lavigne t-shirt, a long flowing coat, gloves with worn out fingertips, a backpack thrown over her shoulder, and hiking boots. Her blonde hair held back by the two braids on either side of her head bounced with each step as she walked across the lobby.

Without breaking stride from the Uber to the Information desk, she walked up to the information desk and stated, "I am here to see Olivia Montegue."

The slightly overweight but highly energetic elderly woman smiled and then started typing instructions into the computer. She stopped, took a deep breath, and looked up to make eye contact with Jenna, and stated, "I am sorry, but there has been a restriction placed on her room. I need to verify if you are on the list, and then your identity, before we can let you up to see her."

"What is going on?" asked Jenna.

"Nothing horrible. They have moved her to the secured intensive care floor, because of her connection with an ongoing case, and by the request of Chief of Detectives Cleopatra Montegue."

"I understand," Jenna replied.

The information desk attendant continued before Jenna could say anything, "May I ask who you are, and can I verify your I.D.?"

"Absolutely," she responded as she pulled her backpack around, set it on the counter, and started rummaging through it. "My name is Jenna Arton." She paused as she found her wallet, pulled it out of her bag, and handed her I.D. to the information desk attendant.

She took her I.D., typed it into the computer, and it confirmed her identity. Handing back the I.D. while the computer created her a pass to access the elevator to the secured intensive care floor. Once it finished, the card ejected, and the receptionist handed it to Jenna. As Jenna took it from her, she continued, "Now you call the elevator to go up. Once inside, you press the button marked S.I.C., and then it will ask for the pass. Slide the pass into the slot with the light on above it. Once the light goes green, it will ask for your I.D., slide it through the reader, and then it will take you to the Secured Intensive Care floor, or S.I.C.. Now be careful, if you lose the pass, they will not grant you access to the room."

"I understand," Jenna replied as she put her wallet in her backpack, slung it back over her should, and held on to the pass and her I.D.. She smiled, went to the elevator, and called it to pick her up. Following the instructions precisely, the elevator took her up to the eleventh floor or the Secured Intensive Care wing. Once the doors opened, she took another deep breath before taking a step out onto the floor.

Hospitals always freaked her out, and the thought of her closest friend possibly fighting for her life made it ten times worse. The elevator closed behind her and startled her into action, and she walked up to the placards with the room numbers. She saw Olivia's room number and followed the arrow towards it. As she made her way down the corridor, she saw a desk blocking the doors leading on further. There was an attendant and two police officers at the desk. She walked up to them, and they asked for the pass. Once she gave it to them, they confirmed her identity before one of the police officers walked over and opened the door, unlocking it with their own pass. She walked through the door and down the hall to the nurse's station. Her emotions were getting the better of her, which caused her to lose track of where she was going, so she asked one nurse at the nurses' station, "Excuse me, where is Olivia Montegue's room?"

"It's just down the hall and around the corner," replied the nurse sitting behind the desk. She thanked her and started her journey down the rest of the corridor. Panning the curving hallway, she finally made it around the corner and noticed a police officer standing in front of a door.

Going for her I.D. once again, the officer held up his hand as to stop her and stated, "You do not need your I.D., Ms. Arton. I know who you are." As she got closer, he continued, "We met last year at the closing of the case where the Montegues found the missing child and apprehended the kidnappers before the child's untimely demise. It was a haunting case. Their family, the child, the city, and I were happy when the Montegues rescued them. I heard you were very indispensable in the case."

"Yes, it was my first case with the Montegue's," she said, smiling as she stopped in front of them. "They are quite the couple."

The police officer opened the door and continued, "Someone familiar is already here. I will let him fill you in on the details, and again, thank you for assisting the Montegues."

Passing through the open door, she immediately focused on the familiar face of her friend and partner in Montegue Investigations. A smile crept over her face as she said, "Mikey." Michelangelo Durelly was a long-time friend of Cornelius. They met in Middle School, and after a rough start they have been close friends ever since. Jenna was one of the four people allowed to call him Mikey, some of his C.I.'s, and the police sometimes referred to him as Mikey the Bull, but all others called him Michelangelo or Mr. Durelly. He was the first partner of Cornelius in Montegue Investigations, but took a smaller and silent role when Cornelius' wife joined the firm and they got married. They all accepted another decrease when they offered Jenna a junior partnership. Jenna remembered what Cornelius said when they offered her the junior partnership, 'Welcome to Montegue Investigations. You are now part of the family, to share in our victories and our defeats. However, no matter what we do, we will do it together.'

Michelangelo got up from the chair he was sitting in and rose to embrace her with one of his engulfing hugs. Rushing into his arms, she could not hold the tears back any longer, and asked, "Is it true? Did she almost die? Is Cornelius really on the run?"

He was a little shorter than Cornelius, standing at a mere six feet even, and despite his constant existence outdoors, he could not hold a tan, which left him rather pale all the time. Maintaining the same morning exercise routine since high school kept him on the side of fit, but he did not have the body of a bodybuilder. However, his physique was a solid, it was his attitude which made him immoveable. A black tee shirt, black jeans, and black boots were his typical attire, as they were today, but when he needed to clean up, he had a couple of designer suits and a fitted tuxedo. His Italian heritage dripped from his very existence, from his accent to the smell of his meatball sub on his breath, and his hug was so supportive and full of love. The only thing that could make it better was the soothing voice of Michelangelo. He helped her to a nearby chair, and sat down next to her before answering, "She made it through surgery, but is in a coma. The Doctors are optimistic she will pull through, but it will be a long road. Cornelius is on the run. They want him for questioning, but we know he will not stop until he catches the one responsible."

"You're right, he won't stop," she answered and stopped as her tears distracted her. She regained control of herself before asking, "We knew the case would be rough, but did anyone think it would get this bad?"

"Cornelius did," replied Michelangelo.

"Really," replied Jenna as she stood up and looked through the window at Olivia lying in her bed. She pointed at Olivia and shouted, "He knew this would happen?!"

"No, of course not," replied Michelangelo as he got up to look at her. "They both knew the risks. She took a chance, and he is doing what he has to do."

"It still seems like an intense price for a case," she demanded.

"The case is much larger than we ever thought. It will take precision, timing, and absolute vigilance to pull this off," he stated as he put a hand on her shoulder. She turned to look at him, and he continued, "He will need all of us when he resurfaces. It will all happen fast, and we must be ready to help him when it is time. However, I promise you, we will get stronger from this."

"But Olivia."

"She would be the first one to tell you to stay the course and prepare for this battle. It will get worse before it gets better, but Cornelius is on the case, which is always the best option for the best results."

She half smiled before replying, "You're right." She looked over at Olivia and continued, "I am going in there."

"And I will be out here," he replied.

She smiled because she knew all too well this was his tone of perseverance, and no one would do anymore harm to Olivia while he was out there.

She walked over to the door leading to Olivia's room. She put her hand on the door, took a deep breath, and cracked the door slightly. The sounds of the machines were almost overwhelming. However, she opened the door further and before she stepped in, she stated, "I will take the watch for now. Go home to your wife and son."

He got up, walked over to her, her determination was obvious, and he was so proud. He smiled and asked, "Are you sure?" She nodded as he added, "I will be back first thing in the morning."

She looked at Olivia before she looked back at Michelangelo and continued, "Now, I have a promise to keep." Smiling as she stepped into the room, she locked eyes on Olivia. Olivia Anne Montegue was usually the life of any room she walked into, from her engaging conversation, her vast knowledge of many things, to her ability to take any awkward situation and diffuse it only to make it better. She would be the first to insist she was not as smart as Cornelius, and he would only concede if she agreed where he lacked, she made up in spades. She always wore boots and jeans with a belt, the fancier the belt buckle the more feisty she would be, but she loved flowy shirts and coats. Her raven hair, which usually made her pale complexion stand out, was a tangled mess. Jenna wanted to fix it for her, but the tubes and wires running to various parts of Olivia made her reconsider. Seeing her friend like this was gut wrenching for Jenna, as all she wanted was to see her vibrant blue eyes taking over the room again with her fiery energy.

Walking over to the left side of her bed, she grasped the chair on her way by, pulled it up to the bed, sat down, and held her hand. Placing her bag on the floor next to the chair, she grabbed Olivia's hand with both hands, bent down to put her hand on it, and stated, "I wish I was there to stop this." She could not help to notice her flawless nail polish, which always matched her lipstick, a bright deep maroon. After a few moments, she sat up, wiped the tears from her face, looked at her, and stated, "A quick update, Cornelius, your husband, is on the run." She looked up into the void of the air above her, and added, "However, before the people listening into this room get any ideas, I do not know where he is!" She took a breath, looked back at Olivia, and continued, "He sent a message to you, though. He loves you very much, and he will see you soon." She fought back the tears, opened the bag, and pulled out the binder she found in the law library. Crossing her legs in the chair, she set up the binder to go across her lap, and looked at Olivia and stated, "Cornelius asked me to get this binder and read its contents to you. He thought you would enjoy listening to it, and I agreed to read it to you."

Grabbing her hand with her left, she opened the book with her right and turned it to the first page.

She read, "I remember all of my cases perfectly, the thirteen as Detective Big Hat with my sister, Cleopatra, helping me along the way.

The five as Cornelius Montegue Unlicensed Junior Private Investigator and, of course, the last three years with you in Montegue Investigations. This is the story which locked my life's trajectory in stone, and I became a Private Investigator. Thank you for accompanying me." Smiling at the uniqueness of the title, she continued, "Cornelius Montegue, Unlicensed Private Junior Detective and The Case of the Displaced Art Class." She chuckled to herself before continuing, "However, for the ease of the reader, I wrote the narrative in third person."

# Some Things of Note

My parents were established people in their fields. Sarah Eve Montegue, Cornelius and Cleopatra's mother, was a famous Christian Authority and Historian with a P.H.D. in History. Our father, Paul James Montegue, had just become a Literary Professor at the local University, and had a P.H.D. in Literature. Therefore, they agreed to pay homage to their professions by giving us names based on favored people in their fields or history. My father wanted to flip a coin to see who would get the first name or the middle, but according to him, my mother gave him a look he described as both alluring and dreadful. So, he said she could have the first names without a flip.

My name is Cornelius Auguste Montegue, named after Cornelius a Roman Centurion considered being the first to convert to Christianity, and Auguste after C. Auguste Dupin, a fictional Detective by Edgar Allan Poe first appearing in "The Murders in the Rue Morgue". I am to attend high school the year after this case, and I am looking forward to it with as much indifference as I look at much of the world. I am considered a misfit, aloof, and apathetic according to many of my teachers. However, they have also stated that I have a unique mind, which was both imaginative and creative.

Cleopatra Shelley Montegue, my sister, named after Cleopatra VII Philopator, the last ruler of Egypt, and Mary Shelley, the author of "Frankenstein". She is one year younger than me and much more popular. I found out she spends a considerable amount of time translating, apologizing, and smoothing out situations for me with our classmates and sometimes adults in my life. For the record, I never asked her to do this, but I have always appreciated it.

A side note: "Thank goodness we did not have another sibling. I could only imagine what their name might have been."

I only knew two of my grandparents, for my mother's parents died before I was two. My Grandmother Jessica Ann (Barrett) Montegue married her childhood friend and sweetheart, my grandfather Saul James Montegue. They were married for thirty-five years before her death a year ago. Six years ago, they declared my grandfather disabled after he was shot in the line of duty and granted early retirement. He went on record once by stating that during his most trying time of life; she was his rock. He also went on record, as stating he never knew going through his disability would be easier than losing her a year ago. He tried to go at it alone but had an unfortunate accident, forcing him to move in with us.

A Final note, I did and do talk like this.

# Grandpa Saul

It was a brisk day in the late of February and snow had threatened to bring its wrath down for the last three weeks, but it never delivered. Grandfather Saul James Montegue, father of Paul James Montegue, and grandfather of Cornelius and Cleopatra had moved in three weeks ago and has been living in the guest room. Paul James Montegue and his wife, Sarah Eve Montegue, had bought the vacant condo attached to theirs and combined them into one house. Therefore, giving them extra space and allowing Grandpa Saul to have some privacy. They combined the great rooms of each into one, kept all the bathrooms, giving them four, and expanded the kitchen. The house was quite livable now, especially since they also enlarged the rooms of Cornelius and Cleopatra. They also halved the adjoining wall in the garage and built a platform he could drive across the garage if he wanted to before going down the ramp into the garage. This was the easiest way for him to get to the street. This gave the Montegues the ability to expand without altering the outer appearance of the house. Thus, making it look the same as the rest of the condos in the Cul-de-sac. They finished a week ago, on schedule, and now the movers could finally bring Grandpa Saul's personal effects from storage. Paul Montegue had scheduled the movers in October, and they assured him a moving date in February would not be a problem. However, after they finished loading Grandpa Saul's things into the truck, the snow that had been threatening to unleash its vengeance did with the largest snowstorm in years.

Over the last three weeks, Grandpa Saul had been spending half of his days between the two different modes: that of the wise old man or that of the crotchety old man. Favoring the wiser version as the day of reunion with his belongings was nearing. The morning shifted from an excited mix of memories and fondness of his belongings into chaos as the movers were running three hours late because of difficulties from the blizzard. Finally, they arrived about an hour and a half later, all because of the storm. Upon the mover's arrival and to the dismay of Grandpa Saul, Paul Montegue, his only son, had offered the movers something to eat and drink before they began unloading. Grandpa Saul thought this was unacceptable, but before he could use his power wheelchair to barge into the kitchen and demand they get back to work, Sarah Montegue, his daughter-in-law, intercepted him and steered him into the study. She closed the door behind them, and within seconds Cornelius could hear her start her speech about manners and politeness. He was glad he was not on the receiving end this time.

After what Grandpa Saul called an unacceptable delay, the movers finished their meal, provided by the Montegues, and got back to work. It took them two hours to unload the truck. Grandpa Saul had them sort his belongings into three categories: First, was the furniture and clothes taken directly into his room, the master bedroom of the other condo, which had a walk-in closet and bathroom of its own. Second, the furniture he had to decide between keeping, giving away, or selling in the cul-de-sac's summer sale. The Final was the sea of boxes filling the second garage, which he had to sort in the same fashion as pile two.

As the movers pulled away, Cornelius smiled as he watched the truck exit the cul-de-sac and turn onto the adjoining road while fading into the blustering snow. He smiled as he thought to himself, 'Thus ending the second stage of Grandpa Saul's integration into our house.' Opening his notebook, he always carried on him, to the list of stages he calculated for his grandfather's integration into their home. The First Stage: his person or the placement of Grandpa Saul in the guest bedroom; the Second Stage, his belongings which were just delivered; the Third Stage, the repositioning of his belongings; and the Fourth and Final stage, the re-establishment of the new norm. Once he checked off the second stage in his notebook, he placed it on top of the book he was pretending to read and the thoughts of all the unattended boxes waiting for someone to look through them consumed his mind. He waited as long as he could, about three minutes, before he decided to disturb the waiting boxes in the garage. Knowing his sister Cleopatra, short for Cleopatra Shelley Montegue, would be furious if he started rummaging without her, he set out to find her.

Several minutes later, and to no avail, Cornelius gave up looking for his ever-elusive sister and made his way to the garage. They were told to stay out of the garage until Grandpa Saul asked them for help, or any of their parents asked them to join them with a similar request. Standing at the entrance to the garage, he looked at his watch, and verified it was indeed twenty minutes after the movers had left. Deciding for himself that twenty minutes was more than enough time for one of the adults to realize they needed help. Therefore, he decided to enter the garage in anticipation of this request. Opening the garage door just enough for him to squeeze easily through. After he made it through, he slowly closed the door, taking the extra time to turn the door handle slowly behind him, allowing him to secure the door quietly. Hopefully, this would assure his parents would not suddenly appear and end his exploits. He smiled as he turned around while scanning the wondrous sea of boxes before him and trying to deduce which boxes might have something interesting for him to discover. He scanned them thoroughly until he noticed one open near the far side of the garage, and his sister, Cleopatra, was rummaging through it already.

Cleopatra was a year younger than Cornelius and had one more year of middle school after this one. Diagnosed with a mild social anxiety disorder, she found solace in her art class, which helped her center herself and tolerate school and its challenges. Therefore, when the middle school announced it would cut the art and music section from the curriculum to meet their budget, she was outraged. So outraged, she ignored the school's plans of also eliminating the school sponsored sports programs and force the students who wanted them to go to pay to play. Therefore, for the last two months, she organized multiple demonstrations around town to rally support with the aid of several other students, the Parent-Teacher Association, and anyone who would stop long enough to listen to her and her supporters. Her platform was engaging and well thought out, expressing the need for students to have other outlets than just a better education and how this diverseness would make them better adults for the future of society. She felt it was a gross injustice to let the students down. However, she always kept her composure as she delivered her defense of the art and sports programs. Normally she would be out rallying people to the cause, but the impending snowstorm kept her home bound this weekend. This would normally have upset her, but she had a sea of boxes to entertain her curiosity, which is why she did not wait for Cornelius to explore them. She was almost entirely in the box she was digging through, when she popped up to confirm it was Cornelius who had come into the room, and once she confirmed it was him, dove back in.

Cornelius proceeded down the ramp they installed for Grandpa Saul and flashed a smile as he looked around at the boxes. As he opened the first box, the thrill of excitement almost got him, until his utter disappointment of his discovery of Grandpa Saul's old clothes. However, Cornelius tended to the side of optimism as he thoroughly rummaged through it checking for good stuff underneath, anyway. Admitting defeat once he realized it had nothing of interest, he re-closed it and moved on to the next box. Again, finding nothing of interest, he moved on to the next box and so on. Cleopatra had stopped rummaging through the boxes when she found the one with Grandpa Saul's old photo albums, and she pulled them out. Stacking them on a box next to Grandpa Saul's old office chair. Once she finished stacking them, she sat in the chair and picked up the first photo album. Without hesitation, she started flipping through its pages slowly, taking in all the memories she could.

Suddenly, she stopped. Staring at one page long enough for Cornelius to notice. He looked over at her and asked, "Is there anything interesting?"

She looked up and froze as she looked past Cornelius, and the voice of Grandpa Saul harrumphed throughout the garage, "Well, answer the boy!" He always had a powerful and grumbly voice, and always just loud enough to be commanding. He motioned the wheelchair to move down the ramp and into the garage. James Montegue, Cornelius and Cleopatra's father, had taped out lines for the boxes to stay in, which allowed Grandpa Saul to navigate through them until he was next to Cleopatra. He stopped, whipped the chair around so he could see the albums, and continued, "Well, what do you have there?"

When Cleopatra let herself get rattled, she would start rambling as fast as her mouth could keep up, sometimes faster, and this was no exception. "I am so sorry for going through your things, but I always loved going through your picture albums with Grandma Jessica. I did not think it would be a problem, is it a problem?" She was about to continue. However, Grandpa Saul had been down this road before and stopped her before she hyperventilated.

"I do mind," he started as he took the picture album from her. He motioned for her to sit on his lap, and as she did, he continued, "I will always be happy to go through these with you, but I insist we do it together, so you have the proper context."

She smiled and gave him a great big hug, and replied, "You have a deal." However, before they started going through them together, she turned to Cornelius and asked, "Would you like to join us? I found an old photo album of the grands labeled 'Our Young Adventures'."

Cornelius looked up from the box he was looking in and responded, "Adventures? Young?"

"Perhaps, after he looks through that box," Grandpa Saul responded as he pointed to the box with his old police stuff, the one with none of his old case files. Cornelius opened it, pulled out some of Grandpa Saul's old stuff: a gray fedora with a black band, a long gray trench coat, a pair of handcuffs, a police baton, and a notebook. Cornelius was excited about the discovery, and as he pulled them out Grandpa Saul continued,

"You can keep them, but the handcuffs stay in your room until you are old enough and allowed to use them. Also, the baton you can have as well, but you may not use it against anyone to you have taken a course at the Police Academy." Grandpa Saul paused for a moment before adding, "And before you ask, you cannot join until you are twenty-one."

Grandpa Saul motioned for him to come and sit with them. Cornelius gave him a hug before sitting in his office chair and thanked him. The sound of pages flipping gently filled the air as Grandpa Saul scanned through the picture albums. However, he did not notice he slipped into his monologuing mode as he started staring at some of the pictures fondly. Tapping them with his hand as he recalled their memories. Eventually, he settled on one particular picture and paused for a moment until he was nudged by Cleopatra. He smiled and started, "I met your grandmother when she moved in next door. Obviously, I would not talk to her."

"Why not?" Cleopatra interrupted.

"Because she was a girl, obviously," he answered with a snarky retort. Cleopatra chuckled for a couple of seconds and Grandpa Saul waited until she was finished before continuing, "It took her a couple of weeks before she got fed up with being ignored. So, she knocked me off my bike with a fastball baseball pitch from her front porch. She ran up to see if I was alright, and after she confirmed I was getting a black eye," he paused as he remembered the moment fondly. "She stood up and said, 'Well, I suppose you deserve nothing less for ignoring me for so long!' I jumped to my feet to yell back at her, but I smiled and outstretched my hand, introduced myself, she took it and we agreed it was my fault. From that moment, we spent as much time together as we could, all the way to the day I got drafted." He paused for a second while flipping back through the photo album until he found himself in uniform, smiled, and then continued, "Three days before I was to report for duty, I asked her father for her hand in marriage, and he said, 'I will not stand in your way, you're a decent boy with a good head on his shoulders, but I cannot give you my consent unless she has agreed.'"

"What did you do next?" asked Cleopatra.

"Well, I was fairly sure she wanted to marry me, but I had never asked her. So, I rushed out of the house and ran as fast as I could to the church where she was attending choir practice. Sprinted up the stairs, burst into the church, ran up the aisle, and tripped on the stairs leading up to the altar. I shook it off, collected myself, and stood up. The choir master was snapping at me about disturbing the practice, but I heard nothing she said as I locked eyes on your grandmother, my Jessica. I walked up to her, dropped to one knee and asked her to marry me."

"What did she say?!" blurted Cleopatra.

Grandpa Saul gave her a kiss on the cheek, then a squeeze, and replied, "Tears were welling up in her eyes as she stated, 'It is about time.' She jumped into my arms, and we kissed. After we took a break for air, she continued, 'And for the record, yes.' Without hesitation, we made our apologies to the choir master and went to discuss it with her parents. We married the day before I shipped out to war. Her parents said they would pay for a proper reception when I returned, and my parents paid for us to stay at the nicest bed-and-breakfast in town for our wedding night. My father assured us we would get a proper honeymoon after I returned."

"I remember the next part of the story," interrupted Cleopatra. "You only kept five dollars at a time from your pay, as you were in the war and the army provided you with the necessities you needed. This allowed you to send the rest back to her."

"Yes, and she worked hard in the factory while you were away. She stayed with her parents, as she saved all the money she could. Combining the money she made, and the money you sent back, allowed the two of you to buy your house when you returned," added Cornelius.

"That is correct, young sir," he retorted. He pushed the fedora down over Cornelius' eyes before continuing, "Yes, the house we lived in until she passed away."

"I miss her," replied Cleopatra, as she curled up into his lap. "Do you miss her?" she asked after a slight pause.

He lifted her chin up so he could look her in the eyes. She could see he was fighting back the tears, and he stated, "I miss her in every single moment of my life. However, she lives on in the two of you and your father." Cornelius got out of the chair, and they all shared a hug.

After a moment, Cleopatra interrupted the silence and asked, "Can you tell us how Mom and Dad got together?"

"Have they not told you the story?" asked Grandpa Saul.

"Yes, but I like it when you tell the story," replied Cleopatra. She paused for a second and added as he conceded, "You make it sound gritty, while Mother's is more romantic."

"Okay," he responded. He took a deep breath and continued, "Well, it all started when I got a call down to the police station. This time as a parent, not a police officer. When I got there, your father was in handcuffs, securing him to the bench outside Detective McCutty's office. His clothes were covered in blood. Detective Paul Stephen McCutty was my partner, and we shared the office, but since he was the senior partner, he called it his."

"Is Detective McCutty, Old McCutty at the end of the cul-de-sac," interrupted Cornelius.

"Yes, but if you want me to tell the rest of this story, I would appreciate it if you did not interrupt," he replied as he spun the desk chair Cornelius was sitting in slowly. "I approached your father and noticed Detective McCutty was inside talking to your mother inside our office. Your father would not make eye contact with me, even when I sat down next to him. He just said, 'I'm sorry', in one of his more hushed tones. I was about to ask him what happened when Detective McCutty called me into our office. I walked in and it was obvious someone had hit your mother in the face at least once, if not in other places. The phone rang as I entered, and Detective McCutty handed me the file before I could say anything as he continued his conversation on the phone. I read it over thoroughly before handing it back."

He paused as he shook his head before continuing, "Her assailant had hit your mother at least twelve times. The blood on your father's clothes was from the other girl on the scene as he tried to resuscitate her after he got the situation under control. Detective McCutty's hung up the phone just in time for it ring again, and he answered it. He spun around in his chair to give him a little more privacy. As he was on the phone, I knelt to hug her, and she hugged me back so hard it was difficult to breathe. She started saying how sorry she was, that it was not Paul's fault, and in the end, she just cried. I told her I was proud of how she was handling the situation and held her until Detective McCutty was off the phone. Grandma Jessica entered the precinct, walked over to your father, raised his chin so she could look at him, smiled, and then came into the office. She took over the consoling of Sarah, and I wrapped her up in my coat. Detective McCutty came around from his side of the desk shook my hand and informed me he had just got off the phone and they informed him that your mother's friend was going to make it, thanks to Paul's timely intervention. Your mother overheard this and stopped crying enough to ask what was going to happen to Paul. Looking out to your father, she reached out and grabbed my hand and stated, 'He saved us, he saved us both.' Before I could respond, she pulled her hand back and curled up in the embrace of your grandmother. Your grandmother flashed a smile of pride and curiosity, but Detective McCutty and I had to talk to your father. Your mother had been living with us since her parents were taken from this world ahead of their time. Her mother and your grandmother were the best of friends growing up and were ecstatic when their children started dating. When she moved in, we set some ground rules on their living together and we made the best of it."

Grandpa Saul paused and asked Cornelius to get him a glass of water. He jumped off the chair, ran into the kitchen to get the water, and returned as fast as he could.

Grandpa Saul took a long drink, and then continued, "Detective McCutty and I walked up to your father. I sat down next to your father and told him the girl was going to survive while Detective McCutty removed the handcuffs. I wrapped my arm around him and pulled him in and held him tight. He returned the hug. I asked, 'Do you love her?' He told me he did. I remember what I said next vividly, 'Are you going to be the kind of person who gets in fights or the kind that will do whatever it takes to make it home?'

His reply filled me with joy and has been forever etched on my soul. 'I will not lead with my fists, but I am glad you taught me how to use them if there is no other option.'

I asked him what their plans were. He told me they loved each other and wanted to be married. However, they decided they would wait until after they had gotten their bachelor's degrees and they married the day after he got his. He paused as he winked at Cleopatra before continuing, "Your mother got hers the year before. Followed by their master's degrees a year later, and the three doctorates after. Two years after their last doctorate, Cornelius came along."

Grandpa Saul paused as he searched his memory, and after he searched what he could remember he continued, "You know, I do believe to this day, he has never raised his fist toward anyone else."

"What happened to Mother's grandparents?" asked Cornelius.

"That is a story for when you are older," responded Grandpa Saul.

# "Do You Want to See My Underwear?"

A few weeks later, just before spring break, there was an incident involving Cornelius and two of his other classmates. They suspended the three of them for the rest of the week and tripled their homework. This punishment was supposed to be stressful, but Cornelius finished the homework the first night and extended his break by another day. Cornelius and Cleopatra enjoyed their vacation with their parents. However, the Sunday before they were to return to school, they bid farewell to their parents as they went out to a dig site somewhere off continent. They left Grandpa Saul in charge and assured them they would be back in a month. After they said their goodbyes to their parents, Cleopatra turned to Cornelius and stated, "Tomorrow is going to be an interesting day." Cornelius half smiled before they went back into the house.

The next day, Cornelius went through his normal routine and eventually started the walk to school with his sister. They were silent until Cleopatra's friends caught up to them and they started catching up on all the information they thought was important. Cornelius watched his sister as they talked to each other, and noticed no matter how much they all talked, Cleopatra was always the sounding board of reason. He admired her for that. As they got closer to the school, the noise from the various students got louder and louder, to the point it would have been quite unbearable if they were inside. Cornelius was wearing the hat his grandfather insisted on him to keep, the gray fedora with a black strip, thus replacing the one he gave him years ago, black with a black strip. None of his classmates paid any attention to Cornelius or made fun of his new hat because they were already used to his quirky behavior and his previous hat. However, Erin Walker, a classmate of Cornelius, caught up to him as he entered the parking lot and walked with him the rest of the way into the school.

Erin Walker stood two inches taller than Cornelius, and as she walked next to him, she liked to stand tall to remind him she was taller. Her brown curly hair bounced as she walked. Her glasses were always polished and perfectly clear. As the wind pushed by her, he would catch a smell of her coconut shampoo. Her excitable personality was distracting, as she would ramble the entire time they were in proximity to each other. She lived two houses down and across the street from Cornelius in the same Cul-de-sac as Cornelius. They met during his first case, "Detective Big Hat and the Case of the Missing Teddy Bear." For some strange reason, since that case, she has determined they are friends, and she even liked him, but Cornelius could not determine the reason. He felt indifferent toward her.

As they parted ways to head to their appropriate lockers, she commented, "Nice hat." He did not break his stride as he approached his locker. However, he cracked a smile and added the comment to the file he kept in his mind about her, "She likes my new hat." This was not unusual for Cornelius, for he had a file in his mind on everyone he ever met. Some of them were so small they were almost paper, while other ranged to double binder size, like Erin Walker's.

Cornelius walked up to his locker, pulled out his books and organized them by order the classes were in. He hung his coat inside, set his lunch box inside, and hung his hat up. When he finished placing everything in their assigned places within the locker, he put all his homework into the appropriate folders for each class, stuck them in his backpack along with the first two classes of books, closed his locker, and went to homeroom and room of his first class. The morning roll call went along as normal, and after the first bell rung and the students scrambled out to head for their first classes. Followed by the students who were scrambling in for this class. The second bell rang while Mrs. Roseland kept telling everyone to find their seats, and once they did, she began teaching the lesson.

Mrs. Roseland was in her later twenties to mid-thirties and stood about five foot eight inches tall. She always wore woman dress shoes with a flat heel. She was Cornelius' homeroom/first period History Teacher. Presumed married due to presence of engagement and wedding ring on her left hand, both in well-kept condition. Has a Ragamuffin cat, as evidenced by traces of fur on her clothes. She uses a lint brush, which he has seen, to collect the fur, but in the spring, she can never get it all. I do not consider her a nemesis, but can be an annoying, necessary evil at times.

Several moments later, Cornelius was drifting off into his own mind, pulled out a notebook from his bookbag unconsciously, and wrote in it between interesting tidbits from Mrs. Roseland's lesson, which he wrote in the notebook he labeled History. However, the notes recorded from Mrs. Roseland's lesson were becoming fewer and fewer.

"Cornelius, Cornelius, can you hear me?" Mrs. Roseland asked from the head of the room. Cornelius did not respond, so Mrs. Roseland got up and walked over to Cornelius. He was writing the prime numbers in order on a piece of paper, which had doodles of squares stacked on top of squares with x's through them, and multiple cubes he drew over and over. On the other side of the paper were complex angles and equation calculations she did not recognize. "What is this?" Mrs. Roseland asked as she took the paper from him.

Forced to stop what he was doing when she took the paper. He looked up at her as she studied the paper and replied, "That is mine."

"I understand, but what am I looking at?" Mrs. Roseland asked as she handed him back the paper.

"A piece of paper with writing on it," responded Cornelius as he took the paper back.

In frustration she responded, "That is not... I mean, what is it..." Pausing as she took a deep breath. Cornelius started running through the options of what she could be possibly thinking and more importantly what she wanted him to answer during her deep breath. However, he did not have time to deduce what she was thinking about before she continued, "You are here to learn history, not to doodle." He put the paper into his other notebook, closed it, and tucked them into his backpack. He slid the notebook marked history directly in front of him to the prime writing position. Mrs. Roseland noticed the pages of notes and how they were only a third of the rest of the classes, and asked, "Could I see your notebook?"

"Of course not," replied Cornelius as he closed it, placed both hands upon it while twirling his pencil between his fingers, and locked her gaze intently.

"I will not ask you again," she stated as she held out her hand for the notebook.

Cornelius flashed a smirk across his face for a second, placed the pencil on the desk, and packed the notebook back into the backpack. While mumbling, "What part of my notebook do you not understand?" Once he finished, he stood up, put the backpack over one shoulder, grabbed the pencil, and asked, "Is this when you instruct me to report to Principal Steven's office?"

Crossing her arms while staring down at him intensely, she replied, "I think you know the way."

Cornelius smiled, shifted the weight in his pack, and walked out of the room. As the door closed behind him, he closed his eyes, took three deep breaths, and counted to four during each breath while enjoying the quiet of the empty hallway. He took three more deep breaths while still enjoying the quiet of the empty hall, he took four steps forward with his eyes still closed. He turned ninety degrees to the right on his heel and counted thirty-four steps, which put him in the middle of the intersection to the primary hub of the school. Taking a deep breath, he opened his eyes, looked down the hall in both directions to ensure it was still empty, turned left, and closed his eyes again. Knowing it was one hundred forty-seven steps to Principal Stevens's outer office, and three minutes before the bell would sound filling the hall with his classmates. He started the walk down the hall while counting his steps quietly in his head. Fortunately for him, he knew it would only take a few seconds to reach Principal Stevens' outer office. He enjoyed the semi-silence of the empty halls and the time he spent on his stroll there.

Finally making it to the outer office, he opened the door, and studied the layout again quickly. From here you could go to Principal Stevens' office, Vice Principal Winters' office, the second entrance to the teacher's lounge and a second entrance to one of the conference rooms, and of course the receptionist's desk.

Receptionist Tami, last name was unknown to Cornelius, was an average young woman. She obviously had some college training, at least an Associate Degree. She wore semi-professional clothes, always practically new and always perfect. Her brown hair pulled perfectly back into a ponytail without a hair out of place. She wore black-framed glasses, had green eyes, always chewed gum, and spoke with a shrill in her voice when she got excited. She liked long heels and to this date Cornelius never saw her standing, therefore Cornelius was unsure of her height. Always introduced herself as Tami, and then tell people how to spell her name, which Cornelius thought was utterly ridiculous. However, she was moderately decent at her job and spotted him the instant he set foot in the office.

Receptionist Tami motioned him to one of the seven seats designated for visitors on the inner wall of the office, looked at the clock on the wall as he passed, and mumbled, "Couldn't have made it to third period, I could have won the pool."

Sitting down in his usual seat, he looked at the clock, and noted the time. As he documented the time within his mind, he pondered on the perfection of the seat and how it was his favorite seat in the outer office, with both a prime position to see the clock and what was going on in the parking lot. Looking over the parking lot and noticing nothing out of the ordinary, he noted the time again before he started looking for the pattern in the floor design. He always thought it was intriguing to see what hidden images in the tiles and never able to find them again, but it was only half as intriguing as trying to find the repeat of the manufacturer's pattern. As he studied the floor, he thought to himself, "Alas, the game has begun."

It was about twenty minutes later, when Principal Stevens came out of his office, saw Cornelius, sighed, and mentioned under his breath he would have to get to him later as he went into the adjoining conference room. Cornelius' eyebrow raised quizzically, as it was not common for Principal Stevens to make anyone wait. Therefore, Cornelius shifted in his chair to get a glimpse of who or what was in Principal Stevens' office. However, before he could get a look in the office, a reflection of light coming from the parking lot distracted him. Looking out to the parking lot to investigate the reflection of light, he noticed one of the three new town squad cars, making the total up to twelve, pulling into a spot next to a car he never saw in the parking lot before. He noticed the plates of the unknown car and saw they followed suit with the other squad cars in town. Therefore, he concluded it was the new car for one of the two town detectives assigned to our town, since it was the biggest in the county, even though they worked for the county and not the city. However, everyone in the city assumed and acted like they belonged to the city as if it were a sign of prestige. It did not take more than an instant before his over analyzing brain had now started the thousands of calculations of why a detective was here.

Two police officers got out of their car, entered the building, and soon after, they entered the outer office. They walked up to Receptionist Tami's desk, who was sitting fully upright for the first time in Cornelius' recollection. Before they could ask anything, Receptionist Tami cut them off and stated, "Detective Harper is in Principal Steven's Office." She pointed the way with an open hand and a gracious smile, with a flirtish smile toward the younger officer which he flashed a smirk back at her. Cornelius suspected this officer might be the mysterious person responsible for the various flowers and candy delivered to her at the school. Cornelius recalled Detective Harper's name from various articles in the paper and news reports from the local news station. He was the older and the first police detective assigned to our town while the newer of the two had only been with the town for the last three weeks. However, Detective Harper had fully embraced the life of small town living and was active throughout the town, although Cornelius has never met him in person.

However, Principal Stevens was in the conference room with members of the school board as she pointed to the entrance. Suddenly, the door to Principal Stevens' office opened and Detective Harper stepped out and said with authority, "I need the two of you to stay with Mr. McCutty while I attend the meeting."

Without hesitation, they stepped into the office while Detective Harper stepped out and looked around the outer office until he locked his gaze toward Receptionist Tami, she smiled and stated, "You will find the meeting between Principal Stevens and the members of the school board." Followed immediately by Receptionist Tami pointed toward the conference room entrance. He nodded appreciatively in her direction and walked over to the conference room entrance.

However, before he could enter, Cornelius interrupted his train of thought and asked, "Excuse me, did you say the janitor, John Saul McCutty?"

Detective Harper stopped dead in his tracks, looked at Cornelius, smiled, and then replied, "Yes." He paused as he patted Cornelius on the shoulder, before continuing, "Now, you do not need to worry about this, son. We have it under control." He smiled at Cornelius and then went into the conference room. Cornelius now could record Detective Harper into a file in his memory like so many others. He was about thirty-five and assumed married, again due to the presence of a wedding ring. Standing about six feet even, his hair and beard were naturally dark brown, and he had flecks of gray in his beard. His suit was in good condition, pressed, and proper. He remembered an interview Detective Harper gave to the town reporter on tv which impressed his father. The reporter called him African American, and he corrected her by stating he was an American who was black. He further commented on the fact that he was no more African American than she was Irish American. She corrected him by informing him that her family was from Scotland, and he thanked her for making his point.

Cornelius got up and walked over to Receptionist Tami's desk, and asked, "What is going on? Is janitor McCutty in trouble?"

"That is none of your business," she stated, while not looking up from her phone. He stood there for a moment, waiting for an answer until she pointed for him to take a seat again without looking up from her phone.

A couple of minutes later, Detective Harper opened the door and exited the conference room. He was carrying a file and knocked on Principal Stevens' office door. One of the two officers inside opened the door, and he went in. Before the door could close, Cornelius heard him read Janitor McCutty his rights, and after he finished, he instructed the officers, "Take him in for questioning, and do not let anyone talk to him until I get there."

"Of course, sir," replied the senior of the two officers. They put handcuffs on janitor McCutty, escorted him to their squad car, helped him into the backseat, and drove away.

Paul Stephen McCutty went into the police force and is the ex-partner of Grandpa Saul. Grandpa Saul always used to tease him and call him the old cliché about an Irishman who became a cop. He married a sixth generation born Korean woman, which upset both of their families. The only one who stood by their side during their entire marriage were Grandpa Saul and Grandma Jessica. They each only had one son, and they agreed to use their children to honor their friendship by naming their sons after the other partner. John Saul McCutty's middle name was in honor of Grandpa Saul and Paul James Montegue's first name was after old McCutty. John Saul McCutty joined the military after high school, and he proudly joined up for another tour of duty. However, during his second tour, he suffered a horrible accident which almost killed him. After his injuries had healed, the specialists had determined he had brain damage, which left him with a difficulty in reading and speech. After several months of rehab, he accepted his new life as a disabled veteran. They had their son late in life and were some of the older parents at their graduation. They were humble people, and even though she died a year ago, she was proud of her son's recovery and rejoiced the day John took over the reins of janitor of the middle school from his retired father. John was a simple, exemplary employee, genuinely nice, extremely shy, and has a stutter since the accident, which gets worse when stressed.

Detective Harper pulled up a briefcase he left in Principal Stevens' office. Set it on his desk, opened it, placed the file into it, closed it again, and left Principal Stevens' office. He smiled at Cornelius on the way out and said his goodbyes to Receptionist Tami. Cornelius kept track of the time because there was nothing else to do, and exactly seven minutes later, the conference room doors opened, four members of the school board exited, followed by Principal Stevens. They all turned to say their goodbyes to each other in the outer office and once they left, Principal Stevens sighed, looked at Cornelius and asked, "What brings you in today?" He motioned for Cornelius to enter his office.

Principal Stevens was a balding man in his late fifties, first generation born in the United States of Greek immigrants. His parents were scientists who became citizens when he was five years old. Slightly overweight but still fit, and his suit has seen a few years of heavy use and patched a few times. Standing about six feet in height, depending on the shoes he wore. He was the Principal of the Middle School in our small town, and lives in the house he grew up in near the university. A patient man, but not without limits.

Cornelius entered Principal Steven's office and sat in his usual chair for a second, realized it was far too warm, got up, and sat in the adjacent chair. Before Principal Stevens sat down completely in his chair, Cornelius asked, "Why did they take Mr. McCutty away?"

Principal Stevens smiled, sat down the rest of the way, and added, "As observant as ever, but that is not why we are here."

"Why are we here?" asked Cornelius inquisitively.

"That is what I am supposed to ask you," replied Principal Stevens.

Cornelius got up from the chair, walked over to the bowl of candy Principal Stevens had on the shelf behind him, and grabbed a handful before heading back to his seat.

"What do you think you are doing?" asked Principal Stevens.

"I am sorry, but the candy is there, so I took it."

"Please, put it back," replied Principal Stevens both sternly and calmly.

Cornelius replied while putting it back, "Why should I?"

"Because I did not offer it to you," replied Principal Stevens.

Cornelius flashed another smirk across his face as he sat down in the chair, and replied, "Then I ask you, why am I here?"

"Listen, it has been an exhausting day, a lot has happened already, and I would appreciate it if we could get to the point? Instead of this peculiar dance you like to drag us through," replied Principal Stevens with a sigh in his voice.

Cornelius knew this would be one of their shorter visits. So, he got to the point and replied, "Mrs. Roseland asked to see my notebook and when I refused, she took offense. Therefore, I am here, however,"

"I see where this is going," interrupted Principal Stevens. He paused before continuing, "I believe you were to make a correlation between the notebook and the candy. However, you are the student, and we are your teachers. Therefore, from time to time, you may have to do something you do not necessarily want to do."

"Even though it is clearly my property," demanded Cornelius as he interrupted.

Principal Stevens rubbed his head as he slumped it into his hands before continuing, "Sometimes, yes." He looked up at Cornelius to make eye contact and only to be greeted by Cornelius staring at him intently.

Silenced filled the room for several fractions of a second before Cornelius stood up, untucked his shirt, and started pulling up his underwear just enough to be visible, while stating, "Do you want to see my underwear?"

Principal Stevens shouted, "No, what are you doing?!"

"You said," started Cornelius.

"Sit down," demanded Principal Stevens. He walked around the desk and sat on the edge while continuing, "Try to understand..."

However, Cornelius interrupted, "I am sorry, but I do not see a difference in the two requests. Either it is private, which the definition of private is belonging to, or for the use of one particular person or group of people only, or it is not. In this instance, I have deemed this private and have not released it for public domain."

"How do you suggest we monitor your progress?" asked Principal Stevens.

"Tests, quizzes, pop quizzes, and homework. I do not see the need to peruse my notebook," replied Cornelius sternly.

Principal Stevens raised his hand to add another point, but instead stood up and told him to wait here. He went into the outer office and told Receptionist Tami to call his parents and left. About half of an hour later, Cornelius could hear the motorized scooter of Grandpa Saul enter the outer office. Receptionist Tami paged Principal Stevens back to his office over the school P.A. System. Another second went by and the door to Principal Stevens' office opened and Receptionist Tami held it open for Grandpa Saul to enter. This was the first time in Cornelius' recollection Receptionist Tami stood up. She waited until Grandpa Saul had cleared the door and closed it as she left. Cornelius smiled as he now gauged her height at five foot eleven inches.

Grandpa Saul guided the motorized wheelchair in between the two chairs across from Principal Stevens' desk. Receptionist Tami closed the door behind her. Grandpa Saul turned to Cornelius and asked, "Underwear?"

"Exactly," replied Cornelius, while looking straight ahead. Grandpa Saul smiled, and they waited in silence for Principal Stevens.

A few minutes later, Principal Stevens entered his office and sat down at his desk. He took a deep breath and stated, "Mrs. Roseland will not ask to see your notebook in the future, and for the record, no one wishes to inspect your underwear." He took another deep breath before continuing, "Mr. Montegue, could you please try to explain why it is necessary to blend into society from time to time to the younger Mr. Montegue." Grandpa Saul was about to speak, but Principal Stevens cut him off and continued, "At home! I will see you on Monday, Cornelius. Please, have a pleasant weekend, and of course I mean you both." He motioned for them to leave, and they did.

On their way home, Grandpa only said one thing, "You know, your father will not be happy about this."

"It is a good thing he and mother are guest speaking at the University of Oxford, in England. After they enjoy their month at the dig site, of course," replied Cornelius.

# Old McCutty's Son

Saturday morning, normally a time for cartoons, adventure, and fresh air, would have to be postponed this weekend for Cornelius had too much to attend. After Cornelius woke, he scrambled to get his morning routine done as soon as possible, so he could go with Grandpa Saul to Old McCutty's house. When Grandpa Saul got up, he got ready to head over to his friend Old McCutty's house rather than his normal morning routine. Old McCutty called in some favors within the court and got his son's arraignment set as the last case of Friday night. Fortunately, his arraignment went in their favor, and they could get his bail set at a reasonable price. Unfortunately, by the time his arraignment had gone through, it was too late to get the money together. Therefore, John McCutty had to spend the night in jail, but at least it was not to be the entire weekend. Old McCutty ran into another roadblock as he tried to collect the money he needed and failed. Grandpa Saul volunteered the rest of the money, on the condition he got it back when he could. Old McCutty was on his way here to collect it before going to get his son.

Grandpa Saul brought the money out of his room with him when he got up in the morning and took it to the kitchen table. Cornelius had never seen that much money in one place before. Grandpa Saul counted the money. After he counted the money for the third time, he placed it into three envelopes and set them on the kitchen table. Wheeled over to the window, pulled back the curtain, and looked down the street towards Old McCutty's house. The rain was merciless and compromising the view of Grandpa Saul. After a few minutes of staring out of the window, his frustration levels climbed until he went back into the kitchen to count the money once again. Cornelius flashed a smirk over the pattern he recognized in Grandpa Saul's behavior. However, before he could open the envelope again, the doorbell rang, and he pivoted his wheelchair toward the door. His navigation was flawless as he went through the house until he got to the front door.

Paul Stephen McCutty, nicknamed Old McCutty, was a detective and partner of Grandpa Saul when they were in the police force for Big City. They had a very good career, helped countless people, arrested many people who needed to stay off the streets, helped those who deserved to get off the streets, countless accommodations, and of course he was the one who arrested the stepfather of Sarah Eve Foster, Cornelius' mother. Their long career as partners awarded them many promotions and awards, both from the department and the city. However, their careers ended early on their last stake out. Grandpa Saul and old McCutty were eating their lunch in their car during a stake out when a drive-by shooter opened fire on them, wounding them both. Old McCutty's wounds went through his throat, while Grandpa Saul's went through his side and lodged in his back. According to the paramedics, Grandpa's Saul's quick actions saved Old McCutty's life at the cost of his own mobility. Old McCutty and his wife always considered Grandpa Saul's actions the most heroic in history. Grandma Jessica always agreed. This ordeal was enough to force them both into early retirement. Grandpa Saul had to take disability while Old McCutty became the janitor at the middle school.

As Grandpa Saul opened the door, his face lit up as he recognized Old McCutty. Old McCutty shook some of the rain off his clothes as he wiped his feet on the mat by the door, and started, "Sorry, I am running late. I had trouble sleeping and when I finally fell asleep, I ended up oversleeping."

"It's alright," dismissed Grandpa Saul as he pivoted his wheelchair around and headed back into the kitchen. He wheeled to the counter where he laid the envelopes.

Old McCutty followed him into the house. Cornelius was enjoying the irregularity of this morning and kept close enough to them to get any information about what was going on without being in the way. Grandpa Saul grabbed the envelopes, pivoted back to his friend Old McCutty, and handed them to him. Old McCutty pulled out an old bank bag which also had a large amount of cash in it and added Grandpa Saul's money to it, while grumbling, "You realize this is only a loan."

"Of course," replied Grandpa Saul. He took a drink of his coffee and offered Old McCutty some. Old McCutty nodded in acceptance. Grandpa Saul poured the coffee and continued, "After all, I am not a charity."

They chuckled at his slight joke. It was an inside joke they always laughed about as they drank their coffee. Once they finished, Old McCutty walked over to the sink, rinsed the cup, and set it in the sink while stating, "I am off to bail out my son. I will call you when we get back home."

Grandpa Saul escorted him back to the door, while Cornelius cleaned the breakfast dishes. As the door closed, Cornelius knew the day was about to get interesting. Cleopatra was staying with a friend over the weekend, so they could leave extra early in the morning to rally support for the Art Department. The business of the McCutty's would keep Grandpa Saul busy for the entire morning, if not the entire day. However, if Cornelius wanted the information he was about to get, he would have to be at his highest level of stealth and craftiness.

A couple of hours later, the phone rang, and Grandpa Saul answered. Although Cornelius could not hear what was being said, he knew it was Old McCutty. He tried to get as much information as he could, reading the body language of Grandpa Saul. However, the phone call was too short to get anything and before he could ask his grandfather what was going on, Grandpa Saul grabbed his coat and told Cornelius, "I am going down the street for a minute."

"To Old McCutty's?" interrupted Cornelius.

Grandpa Saul was about to yell at Cornelius for calling his dear friend Old McCutty, but reconsidered as he chuckled to himself before retorting, "Just hold the fort. I will be back as soon as I can." He almost went out the door when he recognized the look on Cornelius' face and added, "Cornelius." Cornelius did not respond. "Cornelius!" shouted Grandpa Saul and suddenly he had Cornelius' attention again and repeated, "Hold the fort. I will be back as soon as I can."

"Of course," replied Cornelius. Grandpa Saul gave him a look and then exited the door and drove his wheelchair as fast as he could in the downpour of rain towards Old McCutty's house.

Cornelius ran to the door, looked out the window, and after assuring himself Grandpa Saul would not turn around, he grabbed his coat and dashed out the back door. Old McCutty lived five houses down, and it had been raining almost the entire night. He stepped out onto the porch, down the stairs, shifted to the left to avoid the standard puddle at the bottom of the stairs before navigating the yard's array of irregular puddles, to the wall of privacy trees of the first of five yards between Old McCutty's house and his. He pushed through the thin spot he had exploited time and time again.

After slipping through the trees, he took the normal three steps directly into the yard, followed by a zig-zag line through the yard, avoiding the yard gnomes and sprinkler heads that still went off despite the rain, and eventually to the next yard. The next yard took little effort except for the minefield left by Mrs. Einnie's little dachshund. He walked up to the privacy fence of the next house, pulled out a loose nail, lifted the board, and walked in. Walking along the rock garden as if his feet had a mind of their own, or as if he memorized every single step needed to navigate it safely. Through another loose board in the fence on the other side of the rock garden and into the most treacherous of yards.

This was the yard of the twins, Tris and Chris. They were in his class and from time to time and liked to stop and distract him with pointless small talk, which always seemed like there would be no end. As he entered the yard, it was as he predicted and there were no signs of the twins. He sighed in relief as he saw them inside and continued through the yard as stealthily as possible and a moment later, he finally made it to the last house in the line before Old McCutty's, the house with Roland the Pitbull. He reached in his pockets for the treats he normally had for Roland, when suddenly the bottom fell out of his stomach as he realized he left them in his normal jacket, not the raincoat he was currently wearing. He stopped, closed his eyes, and recalculated his path. A smirk flashed across his face as he realized he would have to take the pool/trellis route to get too Old McCutty's. Thus, allowing him to get inside Old McCutty's through the attic instead of his normal route of the cellar. He only had this access availability to Old McCutty's house because Grandpa Saul spent as much time there as he did at their house, and when he was alone with the kid's he would take them sometimes.

A deep breath followed by a well-calculated path, and he was now in Roland's domain. Without hesitation, he took six steps into the yard, followed by a hard right around the aboveground pool, and up the stairs to the deck connected to it. On cue, Roland started barking as he charged toward Cornelius, and in a fluid motion, Cornelius flipped a switch and the stairs raised, trapping Roland on the ground. He walked around the edge of the pool, concentrating on his foot placement, grabbed the pool skimmer, used it as a pole vault, and jumped toward the trellis against Old McCutty's house. He landed on the trellis, slipping for a moment because of the rain as he grabbed his footing. Once he secured his footing, he climbed up the trellis to the roof and into the upstairs bathroom window. It was a fifty-fifty chance the window was open, and he was happy it paid off.

He took his raincoat off, shook it in the bathtub to shake off the rain, borrowed a towel to dry off, and placed it in the dirty clothes hamper. After a couple of minutes, he cracked the door open and peeked down the hall. After assuring it was clear, he walked down the stairs and waited as Old McCutty opened the door and he let Grandpa Saul in. Neither one of them noticed Cornelius at first, while Old McCutty helped Grandpa Saul off with his coat, and Old McCutty handed Cornelius

Grandpa Saul's coat. Cornelius hung it up on the coat hook by the door, and when he turned back, they were both staring at him.

Cornelius smiled, and stated firmly, "Please, act like I am not here. Is this not where you would exchange pleasantries?"

Grandpa Saul and Old McCutty chuckled slightly at Cornelius before exchanging pleasantries and before heading into the kitchen. As they turned to leave, Grandpa Saul stopped Cornelius and asked, "Didn't I tell you to wait at home?"

"Perhaps, but I am here now," replied Cornelius.

"Oh, let him stay. It's not like it won't be over the entire school by the time he goes back on Monday," replied Old McCutty.

They moved through the house until they reached a little dinette. Where Old McCutty already had two cups of hot coffee at the table, one in front of his son, and one he had been drinking. Old McCutty walked over to the coffeepot, pulled a cup from the cupboard, and poured him a glass while asking, "Cornelius likes it black, right?"

"No, chocolate," replied Grandpa Saul.

Old McCutty gave Grandpa Saul his coffee before going into the refrigerator and pulled out a carton of chocolate milk. He poured Cornelius a glass, he always kept a half gallon in the fridge for the Montegue visits. He put the milk back in the fridge and handed the glass to Cornelius before sitting down. They all took a couple of swigs before continuing. "So, what are the charges?" asked Grandpa Saul.

Old McCutty was about to answer, when his son John cut him off, "The... the... they said I sto... sto... stole funds from the school."

Old McCutty put his hand on his son's. It helped him calm down, as it did this time. After a couple of deep breaths, John McCutty continued slowly and purposefully, "The charge is grand larceny, in the amount of one hundred fifty thousand dollars."

Grandpa Saul looked at him intently before stating, "John, look at me." John looked up at him and after a couple of seconds Grandpa Saul smiled, and continued, "I believe you are innocent. However, we have to prove it, that is why we are here, to make a plan, get the evidence, and prove your innocence."

Suddenly, the doorbell rang. Old McCutty did not hesitate as he got up and went to the front door. He opened it and was talking to someone for a moment before the door closed and the two of them came into the dinette. It was a younger man, but older than Cornelius' father. He had a briefcase with him, and when he sat down at the table, he set the briefcase down next to his chair. Old McCutty introduced him, "This is Sam Churn. He will be your attorney, John."

John reached over the table and they shook hands. They both sat down and before Old McCutty could get comfortable, the doorbell rang again. Old McCutty grumbled to himself as he got back up and went back to the door once again. This time he brought an Investigative Police Officer with him, and he introduced him as Investigative Officer Winston Butusov, or as they called him Officer Buttons. He looked as if he was about retirement age and concluded this was Old McCutty's Junior Partner when he retired. Also joining us at the table, he set down a file and slid it to Old McCutty, while stating, "This file has to stay in my presence." He looked over to the attorney and continued, "He cannot have access to it until he gets his official copy." The attorney nodded in agreement, and Old McCutty started going through the file.

Cornelius had never seen an official police file before, and the calculations of how he could gain access to it, so he could examine it, began. After a few minutes, he decided the best approach was the simplest, and asked, "I have never seen a police report before. Can I see it, please?" He scanned the room to gather the tone of the others present before adding, "Under supervision, of course." Old McCutty finished reading the file before setting it down on the table between Cornelius and himself.

As the others started conversing between themselves, Cornelius read each page of the report with insane diligence and committing the file to memory. One report after the other, memorizing all thirty-four pages to memory, and studying the evidence log intently. After he finished, he started studying the evidence again, this time comparing the signatures of the checks John McCutty supposedly wrote. Several minutes later, the detective made his apologies and asked for the file back. Cornelius was studying it intently and had to have his concentration interrupted for him to react. He handed back the file to Investigative Officer Winston Butusov. Locking eyes with him, he asked, "The signatures are identical. Is that normal?"

Investigative Officer Winston Butusov stopped and returned the inquisitive look to Cornelius. He sat down and opened the file. As he started comparing signatures, he asked for a magnifying glass. Old McCutty handed him one he produced out of a random drawer in the kitchen, and the detective began analyzing them in greater detail.

Cornelius made his apologies abruptly, "Sorry, but I just remembered, Grandpa Saul asked me to stay at home." He got up, grabbed his coat, and added as he exited Old McCutty's house, "I should return." In a flash, he was out the front door, ran to his house, went in, took off his coat, and dashed into the garage. Entering his office within seconds, he opened the file cabinet under his desk. His father gave him after upgrading the one in his office. Flipping through the different folders until he found the one marked suspension notices. He pulled it out and put it on his desk and started going through them. A smile flashed across his face as he thought to himself, 'My First Clue! Or is it a hunch or is it a theory? Either way, all I have to do now is prove it!' He pondered for only a second or two while locking this information into his memory and putting the actual files back into his file cabinet.

# My Partner and Friend

Cleopatra had returned late Saturday night from her day and a half of petitioning. Cornelius waited until appointed time he was allowed to knock on her bedroom door, in accordance the peace treaty of last year. She informed him it was safe to enter, and he did. He walked over to her bed, which was already made, and sat down on it. She was rearranging her desk from one optimum setting to another and back again. Cornelius watched as she moved her stuff back to its original placement, stood up straight to look at her progress, and then start over again. Unfortunately, Cornelius knew she was wrestling with a moral dilemma she needed help with but was not willing to ask yet, because this is what she always did in similar situations. Cornelius' sister, named Cleopatra Shelly Montegue, liked to go by the name Cleo, although again according to the peace treaty of last year Cornelius would always call her Cleopatra. She was his closest friend, and despite the fact she was one year younger than Cornelius in years she was more advanced in many other areas, especially socially.

Cleopatra felt as if it were her responsibility to protect Cornelius, even though he was the older sibling. He had his faults, his lack of empathy which she was always apologizing for, and his general aloof and eccentric behavior. It appeared he was not in tune with world as he should be, and she most of the time she was usually correct. However, he showed signs of greatness when you least expected it, he was really smart, dangerously loyal, and could see things in the greater picture faster than anyone else she knew. So, it never surprised her when push came to shove, he always prevailed.

Cornelius smiled as he recalled her file from his memory, she had the largest file in his mind to date. He recognized the note he put in about her straightening the desk when she is nervous, and the countless follow up observations. However, he decided to wait for he to come to natural stopping point and update her file for future use. She was almost as tall as him and gaining every year. Smiling as if it was her natural mode, which he could never understand, and when she did it showed off her dimple in her left cheek. She talked in volumes, especially when she was excited. Her hair was sandy blonde, and she has dark deep brown eyes.

She continued to straighten her desk until she realized she was being watched, in what she considered her lower state, and stopped immediately. Pulling her desk chair to her, she grabbed it, turned it around, sat in it to face Cornelius, and acted like nothing else was going on. She looked at the ground while she took a couple of deep breaths, composed herself before looking up at Cornelius, smiled as she played off what just happened, also the normal routine, and asked, "What can I do for you?"

He played along and asked, "How did the petitioning go?"

She responded with an energetic tone, "I wish it would have been better. We got over a thousand signatures. Mrs. Mindle believes we will have to get a few thousand more, but she hopes the other signature posts throughout town will give us something to be optimistic about."

"Our entire school system is just under six thousand children. Based on the math you just gave me and the totals from the other weekends you have already put in, you should have enough votes, is this not, correct?" asked Cornelius earnestly.

She smiled, turned around in her desk chair, pulled herself up to the desk, and shuffled through one of the four piles on her desk. Continuing through the piles until she found the paper she wanted, pulled it out of the stack, and placed the remaining papers back in their proper stacks upon the desk. She grabbed the paper, turned around to face Cornelius and spiraled the following faster and faster, "I thought that too. However, if you look at how the city's school levy tax breakdown disperses, we must go after the taxpayers as well, because there are more taxpayers than parents. It is all the taxpayers who pay for the school system, not just the parents. It is a collaborative effort of the entire city for the future of society. When you look at it from that point of view, it is a fantastic process in which everyone plays a part. However, it costs more for each of the taxpayers to support the schools and in the end, people dislike to part with their money. Therefore, we have to work hard to show them they are getting their money's worth." She caught her breath before continuing, "It is really hard, and we only got about half of the people we talked to sign the petition. This was the fourth weekend in a row we have been working at it. Hopefully, the ones who did not sign already did. I think it is paying off, and with another weekend we might have enough to convince the School District to put the Art program on the ballot in November."

She paused for more than a fraction of a second, and Cornelius took his opportunity to ask, "Do you think you could relax enough to tell me what is actually bothering you?"

She was about to act as if his question shocked her, then smiled, took a deep breath, walked over to the bed, and sat beside Cornelius. Tapping his leg a few times, before he put his hand on hers, pinning it gently to his leg, and he asked, "Whenever you are ready? However, we cannot address the issue unless you tell me what it is."

Giving him a quick peck on the cheek before standing up and twisting her fingers while pacing. After her fourth trip to the door and back, she turned to him and stated, "Simon and Mikey have returned from spring break." He said nothing at first, until she sat down in her desk chair, looked at him and continued, "How do we prepare for what is surely to come?"

Cornelius smiled before replying, "I have been pondering this ever since the incident and I have calculated several options, which are acceptable."

"And how many that are not?" Cleopatra asked.

He smirked as he looked at the floor, gave a half laugh, before looking up at her and answered, "A few."

She knelt in front of him to make him look her in the eyes, and responded, "A few? How many are beyond bad?"

"That is not important," he responded calmly before getting up. She stood up with him, trying to force him to keep looking at her. Once he was standing completely upright, he tapped her on the shoulder and continued, "I should go?"

Rushing between him and the door, she threw herself at the door to pin it closed as he reached for it. He smiled while resting his arm at his side, waiting for her to give him the normal dose of unsolicited advice. "Please, look at me?" she asked in her pleading sister's voice. He looked up at her and she continued, "We can come up with a plan with fewer unacceptable outcomes if we work together. Now, let us sit down and come up with a plan together, please."

He placed his hand on her shoulder, pushed her gently from the door, and opened it. Before stepping through it, he replied, "I need to change the variables and, therefore, the outcome." He paused as he smiled before continuing, "However, if I fail, we will sit down and tackle it together."

As he stepped through the door, she asked, "What do you think your chances are?"

He smiled as he closed the door behind him and whispered, "Less than twelve percent." Cornelius could hear her straightening her desk as he continued down the hallway. However, he became more focused with each step he took toward his immediate goal. Grabbing an umbrella instinctively as he exited the house, he walked out into the rainy Sunday afternoon, destination clearly locked in his mind, the Durelly household. Knowing it was both the time and the hour he had to talk to Michelangelo Durelly, a.k.a. Mikey the Bull.

The rain continually shifted back and forth from drizzle to steady, but his speed did not waver until he stopped in front of the white picket fence of his destination, the Durelly Household. Staring at the house steadily for almost two minutes as the Corkboard of Complex Coincidences built its files for the house, and to gather his courage. The current occupants were Michelangelo Durelly, also known as Mikey the

Bull, and his mother. The house was a standard Conventional Middle American Home with two floors, assumption of four rooms on the upper floor and a bathroom. It was a dark blue house with white trim and black shutters. The grass was perfect length, marked with one of the local lawn-care company's signs.

After his brief interlude within his mind, he walked up to the gate, opened it, and stepped through. Walking across the perfectly placed pavers making the walkway, he did not stop until he reached the stairs. He took another deep breath before walking up them and straight to the door. As he reached the door, he decided there were to be no more hesitations and he rang the doorbell. While patiently waiting, he shook his umbrella clean and closed it. There was some mild commotion in the house until some steady footsteps headed toward the door. They were female, or at least he concluded based on the sound of what he thought was heels stabbing at the wood floor.

'Therefore, they belonged to Mrs. Durelly,' he thought to himself as the calculations of plausible scenarios started narrowing down. The assumed Mrs. Durelly started unlocking the door's two deadbolts and applying the chain before opening it enough to see who was outside. They locked eyes for a second before she closed the door, Cornelius confirmed it had to be Mrs. Durelly staring at him through the crack in the door. After a brief second, he could hear the chain being removed before it opened fully, and she stepped into the doorway. Opening the screen door so she could see him fully, she stared at him for a few moments until he asked, "Is Michelangelo here?"

As she stared at him, Cornelius drifted off into his mind and pursued the file of Mrs. Durelly. Cornelius knew little about Mrs. Durelly, except for the fact she was Michelangelo's mother. He did not know her occupation, but obviously knew where she lived. She was in her late forties, attractive, brunette with shoulder length wavey hair, and dressed rather smartly. Her makeup was flawless. From Italian descent, as Michelangelo was, and looked as if she was not to be taken lightly.

Once he was done updating her file, he realized she was still staring at him, but once she knew she had his attention she rifled off a few questions, "Why are you here? Isn't it bad enough you almost got my son expelled? We do not want any trouble!"

She paused as she felt herself getting aggravated, collected herself and was about to speak again. When Cornelius interrupted, "The reason I am here is so that I can talk to Michelangelo and clear up any misunderstandings we might have. So that we can co-exist or improve our relations for the rest of the school year."

"So, you are not here to cause trouble," she responded while crossing her arms with the now apparent dish towel in her hands.

"No, I am trying to prevent further misunderstandings," replied Cornelius.

Suddenly, her demeanor changed, and she was delightful. She smiled as she turned into the house and called, "Michelangelo, can you come here for a minute?"

A few moments later, Michelangelo came toward the door and stopped just back enough to stay in the shadows. She smiled and looked at Cornelius, before asking, "Now, I have your word you are not here to start trouble?"

"You do," replied Cornelius.

Turning toward Michelangelo, she asked, "You will behave?"

"Yes, ma'am," replied Michelangelo.

"Great," she started as she motioned for Michelangelo to go out on the porch. Once he passed the screen door, she closed it behind him and added, "Now, I trust the two of you to work this out."

"Yes, ma'am," they replied in unison.

Michelangelo motioned for him to sit with him at the stylish patio furniture his mother was always showing off. Cornelius sat down in one of the two chairs facing a small table. Michelangelo sat down across from him. He noticed a chess game tucked to one side of the table, and two place settings from Michelangelo and his mother's lunch. Silence so encumbering embraced the two as they tried to start the conversation repeatedly, with no success.

Michelangelo Arturo Durelly was the second generation born in America. His father was a career marine, with the rank of Major, and died in the line of duty. One of the three suspended, his suspension was for the three days before spring break, and with warning, his next suspension would be for the rest of the year, just as Cornelius'. Later Cornelius found out they chose his middle name in honor of his father instead of becoming a junior. Finally, after their seventh attempt at communicating failed, Cornelius finally leaned into the table, placed both elbows upon, crossed his arms, and asked, "Do you play chess? Or is that chess game for show?"

"Of course, I play, and I hope you are good," replied Michelangelo as he grabbed the chess set and they started setting up the game. After they finished setting up, Michelangelo grabbed one of each opposing pawns and held them out in closed hands. Cornelius tapped his left hand and Michelangelo revealed the black pawn. They smiled, shifted the board, and Michelangelo made the first move.

After they completed their opening games, Cornelius broke the silence and stated, "We should clear up what happened before spring break." He made his next move and continued, "and where we go from here?"

Michelangelo shifted in his chair to face him, made his move, and responded, "Well, to recap, Simon was the one you were in a fight with."

Cornelius smiled at Michelangelo's move, before replying as he made his move, "Yes, and it was interesting how you, being Simon's muscle, did not intervene on Simon's behalf."

"It was not my fight," responded Michelangelo as he took his next move. Cornelius paused to study the board, he flashed another smile as Michelangelo added, "Check." Cornelius raised his hand to his chin as he intently studied the board, and Michelangelo continued, "Simon had pushed you into the lockers. A crowd of students formed around you to contain the fight. I pushed my way through the crowd and Simon was screaming at you. Suddenly, he closed his fist and hit you. The momentum carried you into the lockers and you bounced off and landed on the floor, but you pulled yourself up to all fours instantly. Wiped the bit of blood dripping out of your nose, and Simon turned to leave as usual." Cornelius made his move, Michelangelo stopped to look him in the eyes, smiled at the move, and continued, "Then you did something no one else had ever done." Michelangelo paused as he made his move before continuing, "You got up. He knocked you down another time, and you got up, but this time you did not raise your fists. Then you said…"

"You can always knock me down, however, I will always get back up," Cornelius interrupted.

"Then he knocked you down a third time. You struggled for a second before pulling yourself up yet again. Simon was going to kick you while you were down, and I knew I had to stop him," Michelangelo paused as his mother asked him to open and hold the screen door. She came through the open door carrying a tray with two glasses with ice in them and a pitcher of lemonade and set them down on the table next to their chess game. Looking them over while she was assessing the situation, she smiled as it gained her satisfaction before disappearing into the house. The glasses of lemonade were already full when she set them down. Michelangelo power drank the first cup of lemonade in front of him, poured himself another glass, as Cornelius took his move. Cornelius reached out his hand to end the game in a stalemate, but Michelangelo politely refused and mumbled through the glass he wanted to play it out.

Michelangelo studied the board for several seconds before continuing, "You can tell a lot about someone by playing chess with them. Which is why I know no matter what my next move is, you have the game in four or six moves. I also knew that I was correct by what I concluded back during the fight. That for the first time in my life, I knew I backed the wrong person, and I also knew I had to stop him."

Cornelius smiled before responding, "Will you accept my offer of stalemate now?" He outstretched his hand and Michelangelo took it before Cornelius continued, "You slammed him into the lockers and that is when the teachers showed up."

They both chuckled for a second as they were shaking hands and accepting the stalemate. Michelangelo's mother came back out. She was holding their math book in her crossed arms and stopped when she was standing between them. Smiling at what she was looking at because she liked what she saw. Looking Michelangelo over, then Cornelius, and then back at Michelangelo before stating, "This is not going as fast as I would like." Looking at them both before asking, "But it is going well?"

"Yes ma'am," they both replied.

"Great," she answered. Looking at Michelangelo, she asked, "Is he as smart as you say he is?"

He looked at Cornelius for a few seconds, before answering, "I know he is."

Looking sharply at Cornelius, she continued, "Then why are your grades middle of the road?" The look on Cornelius' face must have given him away, and she continued, "Parents talk and, more importantly, I listen."

Cornelius paused for a second before responding with a grin, "Then you already know the answer."

She smiled as she placed the math book down in front of Michelangelo and stated, "Then Cornelius can help you with your math homework before summer school becomes your only option." As she went back into the house, Michelangelo apologized for his mother's actions. Cornelius said do not worry about it, and they started going over their homework. Over the next few hours, they discovered a way for Michelangelo to understand math better, and the anger management techniques Father John Ignatius had shown him in fifth grade.

They lost track of time until the familiar sound of Grandpa Saul's wheelchair echoed in the rain. He turned to confirm it was his grandfather and noticed he and Cleopatra approaching. However, before he could say anything, the door onto the porch opened again, and Michelangelo's mother came out and announced she invited them to dinner. Cornelius got out of his chair and helped Cleopatra open the portable ramp they brought so Grandpa Saul could get up the porch. After they set the ramp up, Michelangelo jumped into the rain to help push Grandpa Saul up the ramp and the three of them did. Cornelius and Michelangelo were in the back, while Cleopatra pulled from the front. Once Grandpa Saul was up on the porch, Cornelius and Cleopatra packed up the ramp and put it back in the pocket on the back of his chair. Mrs. Durelly held the door open for Grandpa Saul and they went inside as she stated dinner would be ready in twenty minutes.

Cornelius, Michelangelo, and now Cleopatra went back to the table to resume the math homework. Cornelius found a chair for her, as Mrs. Durelly shouted for Michelangelo. He ran into the house and came back out with another glass. Michelangelo walked over to the pitcher, poured some lemonade into the extra glass, and handed it to Cleopatra, while stating, "It is homemade. I made it this morning, and hope you like it." Cornelius pulled up the chair, she sat down and smiled as she stated sarcastically, "I am glad no one decided to eat the other."

They all laughed before she continued, "Tell him the birth of the Corkboard story!"

"After we eat," replied Cornelius.

# The Corkboard of Complex Coincidences

They enjoyed the splendid meal of Mrs. Durelly's fabulous and coveted home cooking. While they ate, Grandpa Saul shared funny stories of his days on the police force while Mrs. Durelly shared some embarrassing stories of Michelangelo. Once they finished eating, laughing, and bonding, the three children cleared the dinner table, as Mrs. Durelly prepared some of her homemade rainbow sherbet for dessert. The three children got their portion and were shooed out to the porch to eat it, as the adults continued their conversation inside. Cornelius, Cleopatra, and Michelangelo went back to the seats they were sitting in before dinner. However, before they all got comfortable in their chairs, Cleopatra demanded, "It is time for the story of 'The Birth of The Corkboard of Complex Coincidences'!"

"Please, tell us," Michelangelo agreed as he sat down in his chair, knowing this could embarrass Cornelius or give him insight toward his uniqueness.

Cornelius took a deep breath and started,

"It started during the last time I got sent to recess detention back in grade school, almost three years ago. Recess detention had become part of my normal routine, and after lunch, I would report to the band room. Our principal, Father Ignatius, would come in, open his lunch, eat it, and once he finished, he would carefully put his lunch remains back on the tray. He would get out a notebook and pen, clear his throat, and while turning toward me he would ask, "Where did we leave off?" I would remind him we were discussing anger control techniques and how we did not make any progress. He would smile before confirming with himself and go over the three lessons once again. These three lessons took me awhile to fully understand but later in life, I would incorporate these lessons into my personal rules.

First, Peace of Mind, is the only possession that truly belongs to yourself. Allowing someone to get me angry was the same as giving it to them for free.

Second, Practice the Pause. In a nutshell, take a pause before you act, especially if caused by emotion.

Finally, Find the Cause, if you are getting angry, take a moment to find the actual emotion causing your shield of anger to be raised. Once you find the true emotion embrace it and deal with it.

Followed would be a series of exercises and scenarios he would have me act out. However, this day was different..."

I was already waiting in the band room, in the school's basement, where the windows would catch glimpses of the children playing on the playground during recess. However, this never concerned me as I was busily analyzing everything in the room. It was a rather creepy setting with all the lights out except the one over the teacher's desk. It gave both a damp and imposing atmosphere. I could have easily turned the lights on. However, the comparison of data from the two different states of the room was intriguing. A few moments later, Father Ignatius came in silently and apparently was watching me for several moments before he cleared his throat. I turned around, he smiled, and motioned for me to sit down opposite him at the teacher's desk.

Father John Ignatius was in his late fifties and the principal of the town's elementary school for the last ten years. He had a full head of hair which was dark brown but has turned mostly gray. When he was in college, before he found his calling in the church, he injured his knee playing football, and now it continued to cause him problems in his later years. Someone in the parish gave him an ornate black cane with a silver handle to use. He tried to sell it a few times to help the poor, but no one in town would buy it, instead wherever he went to sell it would give him his asking price as a donation instead. He found a personal interest in me, which I later discovered was because of his friendship with my father, Paul James Montegue. They met in college, became friends, and remained so to this day. I would also find out later that not only was Father Ignatius trying to help me, but my father was in on the plan as well.

Before Father Ignatius sat down, he turned the lights on and said, "That's better." Flashing his cheesy smile, he walked over to the teacher's desk, pulled the teacher's chair around, placed it in front of me, and sat down. He put my file folder down, and started, "I have talked to your teachers, some of the staff, and compiled some of my own observations." He waited for me to interject, and when I did not, he continued, "It appears, when you focus, you are one of the brightest students in your class. Your polite most of the time and never back down from helping others. However, for most of your time here, you seem to lack drive and are happy to drift along aimlessly. Is this true?" Waiting patiently for several more moments before continuing, "Let's try this from a different point of view."

He walked over to the door, opened it, and Mr. Dean walked in. Carrying several books with him, he walked over to the desk, opened it, and started leafing through a lot of the pages. He finally found the page he was looking for, and he took a piece of paper from the desk. As he was writing some things on the paper, Father Ignatius continued, "I have a feeling what we are about to do will help you in the long run, but it may be a bit unorthodox." I raised an eyebrow, and it caught his attention. He smiled as he continued, "Hold on a second."

Walking across the room, he pulled over an easel, grabbed a corkboard, and put it on it. He pulled out a package of index cards, a pen, and a box of thumb tacks from his pocket and set them on the table. He sat down and looked at me, and stated, "This is where it gets interesting." Pausing for a moment before he turned it over to Mr. Dean.

Mr. Dean was the middle school counselor who would help at the three elementary schools in town when needed. He was also president of the reading club in the three elementary schools and the town library. I knew little about him since he was only at my school once a month. Therefore, I had little information to base his responses on and would have to take the information he was about to get at the beginning of Mr. Dean's file. Mr. Dean started, "I would like you to read the following six pages and then answer these questions." He slid the paper he was writing on toward me and smiled.

Reluctantly, I read the assigned pages and answered the questions. I handed them back the paper and waited for them to go over the results. When they finished, they looked at each other, and Mr. Dean started going through the desk. He did not find what he was looking for and whispered into Father Ignatius' ear. Father Ignatius replied, "There is one on my desk." Mr. Dean excused himself and left the room, stating he would be back soon.

Father Ignatius smiled and stated, "Well, while we wait. I would like to go over the next exercise." He opened the index cards and placed them in front of me. Giving me the pen, he smiled, and continued, "Write the first twenty things going through your mind on the index cards." He stopped me before I could write anything down, and continued, "Sorry, I was not done. I would like you to write the first twenty things going through your mind on the index cards, but only put one thing on each card."

I was now intrigued, so I filled out the cards and gave them back to Father Ignatius. As he went through them, Mr. Dean returned, and he was carrying a ruler. Father Ignatius held up his hand, signifying him to wait for a minute as he went through the cards. After he finished perusing them, he shuffled them, and then he picked up the package of thumbtacks. He handed them back to me along with the thumbtacks and asked, "Could you arrange these on the corkboard?"

I got up and did as he asked. After I finished, Father Ignatius got up and looked at them for a moment. After he finished, he turned to me and asked, "I would like you to start over. However, this time, let your instincts take over, instead of sorting them the way you think we want you to."

After a few minutes, I finished, and he asked me, "Why did you put them in this particular order?"

"They are in harmony," I replied. He asked me to turn around and asked me where each card was. I told him where each card was and exactly why they were there.

He turned me back around and replied, "Excellent. I would like you to continue this exercise and write down as many of the things going on in your mind as you can in the next five minutes." I did as he asked, and when I was done, he asked me to put them on the corkboard again. There were over forty items plus the ones from just a moment ago. Now looking at the board, he continued, "This is amazing! And this is what you think about all the time?"

"No," I replied.

"No, what do you mean?" asked Father Cornelius.

"This is all I could write down in five minutes," I replied.

"Excellent," he replied as he studied the board. After a couple of seconds, he continued, "You do have a brilliant mind, but I am confused on why some of these index cards are repeated but in different groups."

"Cross-referencing," I replied.

He laughed to himself for a second, went and got another corkboard, and placed it in front of the other. Smiling at Cornelius he continued, "Your first corkboard is great but this one is to be sorted for your cross-referencing preferences."

I continued to stare at the corkboard for two minutes, so I was told, before I smiled, and asked, "There can be more than one corkboard?"

Father Ignatius was getting excited now, and continued, "Yes, but they are all in your mind and you can use different color strings to link the corkboards to each other by their cross-references.

"String," I mumbled as I was still staring at the corkboard.

Father Ignatius snapped him out of his starring state, and finished, "There can be as many as you like. Whatever it takes to maintain the harmony, trust in it, and it will guide you." He patiently waited for a response before asking, "Do you understand?"

"Yes," I replied.

"Now, before I turn this back over to Mr. Dean, I need you to remember this all takes place in your own mind, and you are the one in charge of the harmony and you are the only one that can change its flow."

As I pondered what Father Ignatius showed me, Mr. Dean was ready and asked me to read the same six pages again, but this time, he had me use his ruler. I put the ruler under the line I was reading, moving it ahead of me as I read. To my surprise, it allowed me to retain the information I was processing. Upon conclusion, he asked me to retake the test, and when I finished, they compared the tests. They showed me the change in results and asked me to practice this for the next few months. I agreed, and Father Ignatius told me I could go to the rest of recess. However, before leaving the band room, he informed me, "You do not need a physical corkboard, because your mind can create an infinite amount of them." He paused as he looked at me for a few seconds, before adding, "I believe you have already created them, but now it is time for you to take control of them. Just remember to have faith and find the harmony."

I left the band room and walked out into the courtyard where my classmates and I had recess. As I walked out into the playground, I could visualize the index cards, and to my surprise, dozens of corkboards appeared, all with different headings. Upon filling out the index card, I would place it on the appropriate corkboard, and to my fascination, it would also appear on any corkboard with the coordinating information highlighted on it. It was true, I had already created the corkboards, but I needed someone to guide me to them, and the Corkboard of Complex Coincidences was born. Types of Corkboards Created: Dossier Files, Location Files, Secret and Non-Secret Organizations, Clothes Manufacturers, Clothes Patterns, and later Case Files plus thousands of other things. Including specific things for our school, such as Sports Participants, non-Secret Organizations, the confusing mystery of Cheerleaders, Un-Cool Kids, and Secret Organizations. Noticing everything and documenting it all, thus building the largest database of trivial and meaningful things to cross-reference when I needed to find the pattern wherever it arises.

A moment passed as Cornelius came back to the present on Michelangelo's porch, and they smiled at each other and laughed a little.

After they got it out of their system, Cornelius continued, "That is a fraction of the categories created by the corkboards. One day I counted them, and I realized I created over seventy-four stable and commonly referred to corkboards in that afternoon. It also turned-out Father Ignatius was working with my father, and they came up with the corkboard strategy together." Cornelius paused before continuing, "However, it is time to discuss the here and now, but more importantly where do we go from here?"

Michelangelo stood up, walked over to Cornelius, outstretched his hand, and stated, "You helped me understand my math homework, and I will need a lot more help with this." He paused as Cornelius grabbed his hand. While shaking hands, Michelangelo continued, "My father told me before he died, 'That you are lucky to meet a few good men in your lifetime and if you do, do not let them out of your life.'" He smiled and turned the handshake into a hug while adding, "I believe I have found my first."

Cornelius responded, "I accept your friendship and shall update my files on you." He waited a few more seconds and asked, "Please, can this be the end of the hug?"

# <u>My First Official Case</u>

Monday morning, the most dreaded day for most people arrived, and Cornelius' alarm went off, as usual. Cornelius shut it off after the second ring, as he did every morning since he got the alarm. Sitting up in bed for a few minutes as he went through his normal boot up process until he was fully awake. He jumped out of bed, went to the restroom per his typical morning routine, got dressed, gathered his books while putting them in his backpack, and went down to breakfast. Setting his backpack down in its typical spot by the door, he took a deep breath before turning around and heading into the kitchen. He took his normal seat, noticed the normal cereal he ate every morning was not waiting for him, and smiled as he realized his parents were still on their trip. He got up and retrieved the cereal he needed, and everything he needed to eat it. After eating his cereal, he cleaned up his dishes and everything back into their places. He looked around the kitchen to see if there was anything else he had to do before leaving, concluded there was nothing else, and started on his way to school. Grabbing his backpack and throwing it over his right shoulder, he exited the house. Cleopatra had left with her friends already, so he locked up the doors and made his way to school. A few feet from the porch, he realized this was the first day back at school since the fight and their partial suspension. He assessed the day so far, the delay in the cereal and his normal routine plus his return from partial suspension, and concluded this would be a long day.

They only lived five blocks away from the middle school, and the walk was quite invigorating. Especially in the brisk spring morning. The day was clear and beautiful. A breeze caressed his path, giving him a chill from time to time, keeping his mind engaged with the potential outcomes of the day. Stopping when he circled the last corner, and the middle school was in full view. He took a deep breath, cleared his head of all possibilities, and focused on staying in the moment before taking another step toward school. A few moments later, he started blending in with the rest of his classmates and poured into the doors until stopping at his locker. After opening it, he started placing his books in the locker. At the beginning of each semester, he assigned positions in his locker to each of the books, notebooks, pencils, etc. He smiled at the organization skills he credited himself with and put them in their assigned places. After he rested for half a second, he put his coat and hat in their assigned places. Once everything was in their correct place, he grabbed the books and notebooks he needed for the classes before lunch and put them back into his backpack. Again, his backpack had assigned places for everything, and he put them into their assigned places. Smiling at his daily achievement, he closed the locker and went to his first class.

As he approached homeroom class to check in, Michelangelo merged into the doorway with him simultaneously, forcing them to pause for a second, and acknowledge each other before entering. They decided to keep their new friendship/partnership under wraps for now. Quickly deciding that Michelangelo should enter first, Cornelius motioned for him to go first, and he did. Cornelius took a deep breath and entered the classroom. Acting as if nothing was out of the ordinary, and simultaneously worrying if everyone in class would make him more of an outsider than before because of his suspension, he went to his desk.

The class was continuing as if nothing had ever happened, until the teacher came in and asked Cornelius, "Did you enjoy your extended break?" After waiting for a few seconds and getting no response, the teacher continued, "I believe you have extra homework for me?" Cornelius said nothing, reached in his bag, pulled out his suspension homework and handed it to the teacher. The teacher smiled, before continuing, "I see you gave me all the extra homework, even from the other teachers." Pausing as he looked at it for a moment, smiled, and continued, "Don't worry, I will make sure the rest of the teachers get their assignments." The rest of the class went along as usual, both informative and monotonous.

It was also of note, Simon was not in attendance as he usually was, however, he arrived twelve minutes late and almost received another detention. The class ended, and Simon zipped out before anyone could talk to him. The rest of the class filed out into the hallway as normal. Girls paring up to talk about whatever it was they talked about. The Jocks to talk about sport stuff. Finally, the groups of friends who just were in the same class and wanted to talk to each other.

Cornelius realized he forgot something in his locker and made an unscheduled stop before the normal lunch stop. He had allotted extra time for such oversights and made his way back to his locker. He got to his locker, opened it, immediately found what he was looking for, and closed it in preparation to get back on schedule. When he closed it, Simon was standing there, ready to confront him. Instead, to his surprise, Simon reached out his hand, Cornelius reluctantly took it, and Simon stated, "I hope we can let the past stay in the past." Cornelius flashed a grin, which Simon took as confirmation before continuing, "Great, I hope the rest of our year is uneventful, and we can have a fresh start in High School." Simon smiled like a congressional representative, then let go of Cornelius' hand, and walked into the crowd within the hallway. After the unusual encounter with Simon, Cornelius refocused on surviving the rest of the day. However, as fate would have it, as well as teens, life is constantly developing with intrigue and conspiracies.

The rest of the morning was uneventful, and Cornelius sighed in relief when it was finally time to go to lunch. On his way, he noticed Simon yelling at Michelangelo and eventually pushing him away, as much as he could, and stomped off. As Simon turned away, he noticed Cornelius and came up to him. Stopping just in front of him, he wound up to start screaming at Cornelius, but stopped himself by pausing and taking a couple of deep breaths. After composing himself, Simon smiled and stated, "So the two of you are friends now." He straightened out the collar on Cornelius' shirt and continued while barely containing his anger, "Good luck with that walking Teddy Bear!"

Cornelius walked up to Michelangelo, who apologized, "I am sorry I let out we were friends, but he was bad-mouthing you and I could not stand idly by."

"I am glad. In retrospect, it was juvenile to act like it was a secret and we should take things head on," replied Cornelius. He paused before continuing, "From this moment forward, we take things head on, as partners, and whatever lies ahead. Agreed?"

"Agreed," replied Michelangelo.

Cornelius smiled and stated, "Let's go to lunch."

After they got their food, they sat down and started eating it. About halfway into their meal, Erin Walker sat down across from him. She lived in the same cul-de-sac as Cornelius. She was about average height for eighth grade. Her hair was just short of the small of her back and was the perfect shade of brown. She liked to run with her father for exercise, hoping to join the cross-country team in high school. She wore glasses and was top of the class in grade point average. They met a few times in the cul-de-sac but had become friends after he helped her with a case four-years prior.

As Erin sat down, Cornelius flashed a half smile at her before continuing eating his food. Erin pulled out a notebook from her bag, set it on the table, and begins doodling in it as she waited for Cornelius to finish his lunch. Cornelius watched as she doodled aimlessly for a while until he could not take it any longer. He set his silverware on his tray, cleaned his mouth with the napkin he got with his food, and then set it down next to his tray. Smiling at her, he stated, "How I appreciate a good sketch. I cannot stand aimless doodling. Also, your presence at the table I am eating at is not a coincidence. So, either you have something to ask me, or you have a problem with something or someone you need help with."

"Still quirky," she responded as she set the pencil down.

"Yes," he responded. He paused as she composed herself before continuing, "So, how can I help?"

Not trying to cry, she stated, "I have spent a lot of time on my Science Report and Experiment for this week's Science Fair. I almost perfected it, and when I went to work on it this morning, it was gone. I did not move or hide it, because I thought it was not ready or sabotage myself to buy more time to finish it. Also, I did not move it to be in a better viewing area."

"I am sorry," started Cornelius before she cut him off.

"These are the questions I have already answered," she started as she took another moment to calm down. She continued, "The Pre-Walk for the Science Fair begins tomorrow, and if it is not in place by the end of the first day." She paused for a second to compose herself before continuing, "I could lose my first chance at a scholarship, or worse, get my first poor grade in a class."

Cornelius smiled before continuing, "What was the timeframe of the incident?"

She smiled and added, "I dropped it off this morning, went to my locker, then homeroom, and when I made it back to it, it was gone."

"You are sure the project is sound?" asked Cornelius.

"The report and the science check out. However, I could not get the device to work properly. Therefore, I was going to check on it, to see if I could get it to work."

"When was this?" asked Cornelius earnestly.

"Second Period," she responded instantaneously.

"Alright then," Cornelius replied. He stood up and continued, "The next logical step is to get to the scene of the incident."

She smiled in delight, knowing he was going to help her again. They gained the necessary hall passes and made their way to the multi-purpose room where the Science Fair projects were. Entering the room, they noticed many of their classmates running around checking on their science projects. However, they only hesitated for a second before Erin started showing them the way to her project. Once they made it to her assigned spot, they began looking around to find any kind of clue, but they could not find any. After a few moments, the teacher in charge of the Science Fair, Mrs. Smith, walked over to them and stated, "I am sorry, but your display is nowhere to be seen."

"Is there a way to get an extension?" asked Michelangelo.

"Of course," Mrs. Smith replied. She paused as she placed her hand on Erin's shoulder before continuing, "I can give you an extension, but I cannot call the committee back that could give you the scholarship. You must have it in place by the end of school tomorrow to get judged and be eligible for the scholarship. I am sorry, but those are the rules." She tapped her on the shoulder once again before walking away.

Another teacher stopped Mrs. Smith. However, they were still in range for Cornelius to overhear the other teacher say, "I hope this was not a veil attempt to hide her progress."

Mrs. Smith responded, "That is not in her nature."

Cornelius looked at Erin, and stated, "There is something definitely wrong here. I will take the case." They were about to turn and leave when Cornelius added, "Erin, could you get a copy of the report if you have to?"

"Of course, I always back up my copies," Erin responded cheerfully.

"Excellent," replied Cornelius. He paused as he did some quick math about the next several steps he had to perform. Smiled as it came together, and he stated before he darted off, "Great, you reprint the report, and we will see what we can find."

# Gathering of Evidence

Cornelius and Michelangelo came up with a plan that would require some well-timed moments, and a little creativity. They knew the way to maximize their impact on the case was to not let time get too far away from them. So, they would have to execute their plan this very afternoon, and if luck, perseverance, and deduction were on their side, they could achieve their goals. Now, all they needed was excuses to stay after school, Michelangelo had basketball practice and Cornelius conveniently landed yet another after school detention. After detention, Cornelius went to his locker, opened the floor of it, and pulled a set of keys before heading to the boy's restroom. Once Michelangelo finished basketball practice, he got cleaned up and exited the locker room with the rest of the team. However, instead of leaving the building like the rest of his team, he turned and met Cornelius. At their appointed time, Cornelius left the restroom and arrived at the agreed upon hallway junction just in time to meet Michelangelo. They stopped just before they collided, shook hands for a brief second, and started down the hall. Cornelius smiled as he stated almost excitedly while shaking the keys, "We now have untethered access to the school and can move around freely. Luckily, the sixth-grade choir and band are having a concert tonight, which should give us enough time to find what we need before we get locked in for the night."

"Agreed! Where do we start?" Michelangelo asked.

"The multipurpose room where the Science Fair and the scene of the incident took place," replied Cornelius. Suddenly, he dashed toward the multi-purpose room with Michelangelo in tow. When they got there, they found the multipurpose room doors chained and locked. They decided not to waste time with an attempt to force the lock open and headed to the backstage entrance of the multipurpose room. Darting down the hall quietly until they reached the door, they fumbled through the keys as quietly as they could, until they found the key they were looking for and opened the door.

"Yes," they both said in unison as the door opened and they entered the backstage of the multipurpose room. After a few moments, they were on the stage of the multipurpose room. Immediately after, they hopped down to the main floor, and without hesitation. However, Cornelius stopped them before they took another step, and stated, "I know the adrenaline racing through our bodies during the chase is intoxicating. However, we must show restraint, or we will make mistakes." Michelangelo nodded in acceptance, and they made their way to where Erin's project was supposed to be.

They looked around thoroughly and found nothing. Frustrated, Michelangelo sat down in the chair next to her project, while Cornelius slumped in the second seat opposite him. Cornelius put his head into his hands as he raced through as many options as he could calculate and eliminating them as fast as he could until there would only be one left. When suddenly, Michelangelo added, "If Erin's project threatened us and we wanted to make sure she could not compete in the Science Fair. How would we get rid of her project?"

Cornelius lifted his head to look at Michelangelo, and added, "Yes, and not just get rid of, make sure it could never resurface again!"

In unison, they almost screamed, "The trash compactor!!!"

They snuck back out of the multipurpose room and down to the maintenance room. Sorted through the keys to find the one to open the maintenance room, and when they went to unlock to door to find it already open. This was suspicious, but since they were outsourcing John McCutty's job during the trial, it could be plausible the temporary janitor left it unlocked. However, since the opportunity was there, they went in and look around for the compactor, or better yet, a clue or two. It took only a moment to find Erin's science project tucked under some loose boxes in the compactor. Without hesitation, they dug the project out and set it on the workbench on the far side of the maintenance room. After they set it down, Cornelius and Michelangelo verified it was all there, tightened what had become loosened, and repaired what broke after it was thrown into the compactor. After several minutes, they finished the repairs and were ready to return it to the multi-purpose room. Knowing Erin would bring the report tomorrow, they decided not to look for it. However, they noticed it lying in the waste bin marked for the incinerator, and Cornelius grabbed it before they left. They moved as fast as they could without hurting the machine back to the multipurpose room and put it back where it belonged.

Michelangelo was taking a moment to look at their success with pride as Cornelius started looking through her paper. Smiling as Michelangelo took another moment to savor the victory, before stating, "I have to get going. My mom is probably waiting for me."

"Alright," Cornelius motioned for him to go, as he sat down, and started deep reading Erin's report. It was fascinating and was captivating, and after a few moments, he smiled as he realized how he could help her fix her report. Once he finished reading the report, he went back to the beginning and started making the corrections with the highlighter and pen he always carried on him. Upon finishing the corrects for the report, he put it down next to the project, smiled, and began working on the project corrections. As he almost finished, he paused for only a second, as the thoughts of his help might be construed as interference from an outside source. He debated in his mind, 'After all, this was her project, not theirs. However, it only took a couple of seconds for him to dismiss it as he justified to himself that the best scientists would ask for help when they need it, or work with a team who helped each other out. On the other hand, she could have come to the proper conclusions and fixed herself if she had access to it today to do her final adjustments.'

A couple of hours later, he realized he got fixated again and lost track of time. Knowing the school was locked down for the night by now, and he would have to find a phone to call Grandpa Saul. Smiling as he realized, with the keys in his possession, he had access to the entire school, and thought to himself, 'What a better place to call Grandpa Saul than from the school's office, and how this could become the ideal time to check into his suspicion of the signature on his suspension notice.' In a flash he was off to the school's office, on his way he noticed the school seemed a lot larger in the quiet and the dark. However, he pressed on until he got to the office, unlocked it with the acquired keys, and made the call to Grandpa Saul from Receptionist Tami's phone. He made the call first in case someone caught her later and needed a story to back himself up. Grandpa Saul started going on about the inconvenience of Cornelius' actions. However, Cornelius decided the amount of extra trouble he would be in for what he was about to do was negligible, considering the amount he was already in, and he hung up the phone while Grandpa Saul was still talking.

After the receiver landed on the base, Cornelius immediately turned to Vice Principal Winters' office. Using the keys again, he opened the door and stepped in, while closing the door after him. He started going through the papers on his desk, making sure they settled in the same place as he found them. Finding a couple of samples which looked close enough to his suspension notice, but in the end, he wanted the actual suspension notice to verify it. 'The file cabinet,' he thought to himself as he went to open it. However, his frustration grew when he found it locked. Taking a second to gain his bearings before he started looking for the key.

After looking around for a second, he realized the best spot would have to be in the desk. After he opened a couple of drawers, he remembered people usually keep spare keys or things they did not want exposed underneath or inside something. So, he started looking underneath the drawers and desktop. As he opened the last drawer, he felt a small book taped to the underside of it and reached for it. Gently pulling it off, he placed it on the desktop and started looking through it. Most of it made little sense to Cornelius, as if written in some sort of code. He continued to look through the ledger until he eventually found some pages that coordinated with the dates of the accusations of John Saul McCutty's son.

Suddenly, headlights flashed across the office walls, and Cornelius knew his time was running out. However, he wanted these pages, so he ran to the door of the outer office, locked it, and wedged a chair under it to give him as much time as possible. Once the chair was in place, he started making copies, going from the back of the book toward the front. He made it halfway through the book, when the door finally rattled as if someone were trying to open it. Cornelius watched intently to see the progress of the door as he continued to make copies.

Suddenly, he heard Vice Principal Winters call out for Cornelius to open the door. Cornelius did not respond, but kept copying. A couple of minutes later, he had only two pages to go when Grandpa Saul shouted, "Cornelius, open this door!"

Finishing the final two copies, he set the copier to copy twenty more pages and cleared the history. He overheard Receptionist Tami talking to the I.T. Department on the phone once when he was in the office. They told her to copying blank pages and clearing the history was the only way to clear the copier's memory. While the final blank pages passed through the copier, Cornelius put the book back flawlessly. Then ran to Receptionist Tami's desk and put the keys he was using in the box of tissues she kept in the bottom drawer of her desk. Letting the copier do what it needed to, he walked over to the door, and finally replied, "If you stop pushing, I will open it for you."

Once they stopped, he removed the chair, and the door opened. Vice Principal Winters charged in, grabbed Cornelius by the collar, and demanded, "What were you up to? And why did it take you so long to open the door?"

While Cornelius' shirt pulled tightly around his neck, he flashed a smile, before answering, "Sorry, I saw a scary movie last night, and I was hiding under Receptionist Tami's desk." Continuing with an increasing amount of sarcasm, he continued, "When I heard my grandfather, I opened the door."

"You have your answer. Now put down my grandson," demanded Grandpa Saul. Once Cornelius was on the ground, he walked over to Grandpa Saul, and Grandpa Saul continued, "Thank you for letting us in the building, but I think we will walk home."

Vice Principal Winters escorted them out of the building, locked up the school after they left, and sat in his car watching them until they left the school grounds.

Cornelius and Grandpa Saul did not talk the entire way home. However, once they were inside, Grandpa Saul asked as he maneuvered into the kitchen, "What do you have to say for yourself?"

"I think I found something that..." started Cornelius.

"I am sure whatever you found is interesting, but if I am going to back you up, I need to know where you are before it happens, not after," Grandpa Saul stated as he poured himself a cup of coffee. He called Cleopatra down. Once she got there, he asked her to make herself and Cornelius some hot chocolate and informed her he had already heated the water. After they each got their hot chocolate, they all sat down at the kitchen table and remained silent.

After several sips of their beverages, Grandpa Saul broke the silence and stated, "Show me what you found."

# Principal Stevens' Office Once Again

The following day, Cornelius got up as usual and followed his new normal morning routine, the one without his mother getting everything ready for him. After he finished, he locked up the house and walked to school as usual. However, this time, he met up with Michelangelo after his mom dropped him off. They joined their classmates as they entered school, and Cornelius stated, "Good to see you."

"You as well," replied Michelangelo out of auto-response. As they approached the building, he could not help but notice how tired Cornelius looked, and asked, "How long did you stay after I left?"

"They had to come and get me," replied Cornelius humbly.

"Who?" asked Michelangelo.

"The Vice Principal Winters and Grandpa Saul," responded Cornelius.

"Were they mad?" asked Michelangelo. He stopped their progress to hear his response more intently.

Cornelius flashed a smile and stated, "About the usual level." He paused for only a moment before continuing, "However, that is nothing compared to what I found?"

Michelangelo looked around briefly to make sure no one was around who should not be, and asked, "What would that be?"

"A ledger, but we think it is in code and not complete. Grandpa Saul believes there is another half, and we need the other half to make sense of it," responded Cornelius as they started back into school.

Michelangelo grabbed him by the shoulder and asked, "How did you figure out it was only half?"

Cornelius was about to respond enthusiastically, but shifted gears and replied, "Grandpa Saul figured it out, but agreed the other half would be quite interesting to see."

"Where do you think it is?" responded Michelangelo.

"I think we need to take a trip to Vice President Winters' house," responded Cornelius.

"That sounds like fun," replied Michelangelo.

"Tonight then?" asked Cornelius.

"After practice," replied Michelangelo excitedly.

"Excellent, now let us see where the day leads us," Cornelius replied as they entered the school.

After the ritual dodging of classmates in the hallway and integration with their lockers, they were off to homeroom or, as Cornelius liked to call it, mandatory attendance. However, unlike what they have done every other day when they entered homeroom during their middle school days, this one threw Cornelius for a loop. As they walked in, Erin suddenly appeared out of nowhere and gave Cornelius a big hug in front of the entire class. It seemed like a minor eternity to Cornelius, one he hated and did not mind at the same time. However, according to Cornelius, it lasted the maximum time something of this nature was allowed to by his standards, and he knew he had to expedite the situation.

"I take it you found your science project?" asked Cornelius. He tapped her on the back, signifying the hug was over, and after she let go, he continued, "I have science class fourth period and it will delight me to see what you have to show the rest of us."

She smiled before pulling him in close and whispering in his ear, "I tested it and it works. I have enough time to re-write my report with your corrections." Her excitement was beyond control, and she hugged him again while adding, "Thank you!" She let go and dashed to her desk to wait anxiously for homeroom to be over so she could go and re-write her paper. Cornelius looked around the room for a second to analyze the reaction of his classmates, and according to his calculations, only a handful of his classmates were talking about the hug. He flashed a half-smile. Then went to his desk as if nothing had just happened, waiting for the monotone call of attendance once again. After homeroom was over, Erin dashed out of the room before anyone else even got out of their chairs. The rest followed in their normal fashion, with Cornelius hanging back only a few moments, so the people pouring into the more than average doorway would not jostle him.

Shortly after the rest of his classmates from homeroom exited, Cornelius entered the hallway and made his way to his next class. He was scribbling down some information in his notebook without watching where he was going. Making his way to the next class as if his body knew the way on its own. The next class went as normal as it ever did, and he repeated the same routine from this class to the next. Until he finally made it to his science class, the teacher was abuzz with excitement over the Science Fair and the fact the Scholarship Committee was coming to judge. Cornelius did not even have a second to sit down before the teacher was lining everyone up to go to the multi-purpose room for the Science Fair and giving everyone his instructions of expected behavior for the Science Fair. Once the teacher finished his instructions, he added as a reinforcement to his instructions, "Now, once we are at the Science Fair, we will be on our best behavior. You will be free to roam around and check out the other experiments. I cannot say this enough, so I will say it again. I expect everyone to be on your best behavior."

Cornelius put away his notebook, as he traditionally did for his classes, and followed the rest of his classmates to the Science Fair. Arriving at the multipurpose room, they filed in two rows before entering. This was the eighth grade Science Fair, and the eighth graders were the first ones to see the projects, and they were all freed up for fourth period so they could get in before the rest of the school got their turns. Once they were all in, Erin ran up and gave Cornelius a quick hug before grabbing his hand and dragging him over to her project. "Look," she shouted.

Cornelius looked her project up and down before asking, "I suppose you want me to guess what it is you wanted me to see?" Pausing for a moment before continuing, "Is it your working project? Or is it your newly typed report? Or is it the A+ you got on both?"

She hugged him again, and whispered into his ear, "I know you fixed my project and report. Thank you so much for helping me." Releasing him from the hug only to give him a quick peck on the cheek before she ran off to be with her girlfriends and they shrieked about her grade with them.

Cornelius left Erin's project to wonder around to check some of the other projects. A few minutes later, he came across Michelangelo at his project, who had respectfully scored a B+, and they discussed his project for a little while. After Cornelius gathered all the information, he could from Michelangelo about his project. They made their rounds together and checked out the rest of the projects. Eventually they came across Cornelius' project and Michelangelo asked him about his grade, a 'C-'. Stopping dead in his tracks, Cornelius turned to Michelangelo and asked with conviction in his voice, "I am sorry. Is it not a passing grade?"

Michelangelo was about to follow up, when suddenly Simon was yelling at the teacher in charge of the Science Fair. Unfortunately for Simon, Vice Principal Winters was not here today, and Principal Stevens was heading over to the commotion. Simon was insisting, "I know for a fact, someone tampered with Erin's project. She received the highest grade and did not give credit to the person who helped her. I demand you bring the Grant Committee back to review my experiment with this new information!"

Principal Stevens was now in the conversation and interrupted, "First, you better be sure of who you are accusing. Erin is an ideal student, and her record speaks for her, unlike your own, which is not one I am willing to talk about here and now."

Simon stepped up to Principal Stevens and shouted, "Who do you think you are talking to? I will bring my father down here and he will set you in your place!"

Principal Stevens chuckled for a second. Smiled and then responded, "I am not afraid of your father. By the way, you just earned yourself one of your last three detentions, or do you wish it to be two?"

Cornelius and Michelangelo had made their way to Simon's project and were now in the sight of Simon. Simon paused from his rant for a moment as he stared at the pair. He huffed in frustration as he was calculating his next step, before pointing at Cornelius and Michelangelo and shouting, "It was them!"

They looked at each other, then shrugged their shoulders as they turned back to Simon. Simon grew enraged, and shouted, "It had to be them. Only Cornelius would have found Erin's experiment in the compactor..." Simon stopped shouting suddenly. When he realized he let slip the location of the project, he tried to walk away discreetly.

However, Principal Stevens put his hand on Simon's shoulder and stated, "I am curious to understand how you knew the project was in the compactor. So, if you do not mind, will you accompany me to my office?" He smiled at Cornelius and Michelangelo before continuing, "Of course, this involves the two of you, and now we all shall accompany me to my office. Where we will wait once again for your parents." Principal Stevens made sure the walk to his office was quiet, with Simon in front of him and the newly founded friend duo closely behind.

Once they entered the office, he turned to Receptionist Tami. Her phone was already in her hand, and before Principal Stevens could say anything, she asked, "Should I call all of their parents and or guardians?"

Principal Stevens smiled at her efficiency and replied, "Just Simon's."

Simon mumbled something about it not being fair while Principal Stevens escorted him into his office, sat him down in a chair, and told him not to move. He closed the door to his office as he exited and approached Cornelius and Michelangelo. Smiling as he sat down in a chair to see them on a more even level, and started, "I do not believe the two of you are up to mischief. Erin's record speaks for itself, and since there was no roughhousing, there is no reason for the two of you not to return to class. So, off you go." He stood up, and as he turned to go back into his office, he added, "It looks like I will have to keep my eye on the two of you."

"Thank you," replied Cornelius and Michelangelo reluctantly, before they exited the office. As Cornelius shut the door behind them, he overheard Tami stating that Simon's mother was on the way.

# An Evening of Misadventures

The next day, Friday, after school, Cornelius and Michelangelo met up and started their journey home. However, the moment they left the school grounds, Simon stepped out from behind a bush and into their path. He was extremely calm for Simon, and he walked up to Michelangelo and stated, "You have chosen the wrong side, Michelangelo. We will see who is the one on top by the end of the year." Simon turned and left without saying another word, while Cornelius and Michelangelo watched him walk away. Once they confirmed he was out of sight, Cornelius made sure they were alone, before turning to Michelangelo and asked, "Do you have anything going on tonight?"

"No, why?" asked Michelangelo.

"Ask your mom if you can stay over tonight. We need to come up with a plan to help John McCutty. I overheard something when I was in the hallway in front of the office that might help. Meet me at my office when you get a chance." Michelangelo gave him a quizzical look. Cornelius added, "My garage."

Michelangelo nodded and was off to catch a ride home with his mother and to ask permission to stay the night at Cornelius'. Meanwhile, Cornelius looked around to make sure he was still alone, opened his notebook, and started studying the pages as he walked home. Walking almost instinctively, he hardly looked up from his notebook, stopping at the crosswalks as if his feet knew what to do, and only looking up to cross the roads. Making it home in the allotted time, Cornelius walked up to the garage, typed in the code without looking up from his notebook, and once the door raised, he walked in. Placing his hat on the nightstick on his desk, he closed the notebook and put it in his pocket. He walked up to the landing, allowing access to the house, pressed the garage door button, watched the door close, and after it did, he continued into the house.

Going through his normal routine, until he heard the phone ring, and before it rang twice, Grandpa Saul answered. He listened to who was talking for a few minutes before he grumbled, "Sure, it is no problem." Once he finished the conversation, he turned to Cornelius, and continued, "Shouldn't you have asked me first?"

"About what?" asked Cornelius.

"You know what?" Grandpa Saul responded with a slight chuckle. He turned to go into the other room and continued, "Michelangelo will be over in a couple of hours."

Cornelius cracked a smile and discreetly made his way back to his desk in the garage. About an hour and a half later, a tan minivan pulled up in front of his house and parked. Michelangelo and his mother got out and made their way to the front door. Cornelius reentered the house as his Grandpa Saul was opening the door. They all exchanged pleasantries, Grandpa Saul invited Michelangelo's mother in for some coffee, and Cornelius and Michelangelo asked in unison, "Can we be excused?" Once they were, they immediately proceeded to the garage. Michelangelo's mother followed Grandpa Saul into the kitchen for a cup of coffee.

As they entered the garage, they went down the ramp, which went out from the door enough to clear the door and Grandpa Saul's motorized wheelchair before turning immediately to the right, allowing him access to the garage floor. There was also a short staircase to the left, allowing shorter access for others. They lifted the safety railing protecting the stairs and went down them, closing the safety rail on the way. The stairs were the shortest way out of the garage. Once they were on the garage floor, Cornelius gave him the five second tour, and Michelangelo could tell Cornelius was almost eager to get to something specific in the garage as he ran through the list of each item in the garage. Finally, Cornelius cracked a smirk across his face as he pointed to his desk and stated, "I have saved the best for last."

He took a deep breath and started the walkthrough of his desk. To the left of the garage door, up against the wall, was an old desk with a corkboard on the wall and several index cards pinned upon it. Some of the index cards had string linking them to others, while the rest seemed to follow some sort of bizarre pattern. There was a four-shelf organizer on the upper right corner of the desktop, under the lower right portion of the corkboard. A detention notice was peeking out of the lower middle shelf. Newspaper clippings on the lowest shelf, organized in two piles, only recognizable to Cornelius. Odds and ends on the other middle shelf, and a report with highlights and black lines on it with both the highlighter and marker on the top shelf. He had taped a Police Side Handle Batton to the desk, with the side handle on the desktop, and the long handle taped to the shelf organizer. His new gray fedora with a black strip around the brim was on it like it was at its home.

To the left of the organizer was a neatly stacked pile of blank index cards. A chess board was on the upper left-hand side of the desk. It looked like it was in mid-game. However, there were some pieces knocked over by the copies of the book Cornelius found in Vice Principal Winters Office. The copies were paper clipped together, and mostly in the center of the desk, except the corner that crossed the chessboard. There were five pencils and two pens inline in front of the shelf organizer. A coffee mug with the words "Wake Up!" on it holding tacks in it for the corkboard next to the index cards. A picture of Cupcake, Old McCutty's basset hound, in the middle of the top of the desktop, closer to the chessboard. A notebook labeled curiosities on the lower left hand of the desktop. An out-of-place red pawn chess piece, which was in front of the picture of Cupcake. The rest of the desk was intentionally left clear to guarantee Cornelius had space to do his work, and, of course, his father's old file cabinet tucked underneath.

Michelangelo studied it for a while before asking, "What am I looking at?"

Cornelius stared at him for what felt like an hour to Cornelius, even though it was only a few seconds, before asking, "What do you mean?"

Michelangelo scrambled for the most tactful way to state what he meant, as it was becoming obvious he might have hurt Cornelius' feelings. A few seconds later, he responded, "I mean, most of it makes sense, but, for example, what is the red pawn about?"

"I found it placed perfectly in the center of my available shelf in my locker. I have narrowed the suspects down to eighty-seven," replied Cornelius sternly.

"Isn't there only two hundred kids in our school?" asked Michelangelo.

"There is two hundred sixty-one, and before you ask, I have eliminated two-thirds of the students in school," responded Cornelius.

"Which leaves our entire class?" asked Michelangelo.

Cornelius flashed a quick smirk before replying, "Precisely."

Not knowing if it was a good thing or not, Michelangelo pushed past it and asked, "Could you please walk me through your desk layout?" Cornelius smiled and took him through every index card, copied paper, chess piece, and newspaper clipping. It took a couple of hours and he finished just in time for dinner.

Grandpa Saul made his famous burgers and homemade fries. They enjoyed their dinner, did the dishes, and snuck back into the garage to begin their plan.

After a couple of minutes of debate over their next move, Cornelius broke down, hunched over his desk, and stated, "If we only knew where Vice Principal Winters lived."

Michelangelo smiled before responding, "He lives two blocks down and one street over from my house."

Cornelius perked up and started calculating, before he asked, "How fast can you ride?"

Michelangelo scoffed as he responded, "Faster than you!"

"Excellent," replied Cornelius as he pulled a map of the town out of his desk. He used a ruler and started calculating. After a couple of seconds, he continued, "If we ride our bikes to his house, and we are lucky, we should be able to get the rest of the evidence we need."

"Then what are we waiting for?" asked Michelangelo.

Michelangelo grabbed Cornelius' father's bike, Cornelius grabbed his, and they were off. Michelangelo was the better rider with a better bike, but he made sure they stayed close to each other so they could communicate if necessary. However, their determination and distance they were trying to get to in a short time created one of the most silent bike rides in the history of children. Once they got about half a block away from Vice Principal Winters' house, they staged their bikes behind some bushes and proceeded the rest of the way on foot. In a matter of minutes, they were close enough to climb his fence. Cornelius knelt, Michelangelo joined him, and they discussed their mission. Cornelius started, "First we need to get into his house. Second, we need access to his computer. Third, we need to find the evidence and copy it to this external hard drive. Fourth and finally, we need to get out of there, preferably unseen." He pulled an external hard drive out of his pocket and showed it to Michelangelo.

Michelangelo rolled his backpack off his back and placed it in front of him. He opened it and rummaged through it for a moment until he pulled out a camera and a collapsible stand.

"What is that for?" asked Cornelius.

"Just in case, no one believes two children and what they discovered," replied Michelangelo.

Cornelius paused for a moment, smiled, and replied, "How do we get into the house?"

"I think we should go in through the backyard. We can set up the camera it in wide angle mode, so it can capture the most action on the video," suggested Michelangelo.

"Agreed," replied Cornelius. There was music playing in the backyard as they made their way along the fence until they found a section they could get over. They figured once they landed, some of Vice Principal Winters' prize-winning burning bushes would hide them. They took a deep breath, and, in an instant, they were over the fence. Upon landing, they made sure no one noticed them before they started the next step of the plan. Michelangelo attached the camera stand to the camera, and they set it up between two of the fire bushes. As he was making sure the picture was coming in clear, Michelangelo asked, "Who is that in Vice Principal Winters' hot tub?"

Cornelius looked through the bushes and replied, "That is Simon's dad."

"I can see that, but who is the girl he is kissing?" asked Michelangelo.

Cornelius took another look, and added, "I do not know, but that is not Simon's mom." He paused for a moment before continuing, "Please tell me you are recording this?"

"I am, why?" asked Michelangelo.

"This could be useful. According to Grandpa Saul's old police shows, adults hate this kind of behavior. "

Michelangelo nodded while Cornelius looked around some more to make sure they still had the advantage. Finally, Cornelius spotted Vice Principal Winters, and he tapped Michelangelo on the shoulder. Once he had his attention, he stated, "Look, Vice Principal Winters is on his computer. If we can distract him enough to come outside, I could slip in and hopefully copy enough files."

Michelangelo stated, "Give me a second and you will have your distraction."

"When will I know the distraction?" replied Cornelius.

"You will know," Michelangelo replied. He tapped Cornelius on the shoulder before disappearing into the foliage of Vice-Principal Winter's Garden.

Cornelius moved closer to the house so he could make a quicker entrance, and once he was in place, he watched the yard for the signal. A few seconds later, a lawnmower started and burst from the deteriorating shed in the back of the yard. It was on a crash course with some of Vice-Principal Winters' prize flowers. Vice Principal Winters looked up from his computer and dashed out of the house as fast as he could. Cornelius caught the door before it closed, slipped in, and gently closed it behind him. Moving cautiously, he made it to the computer, inserted the USB cable, and connected the external hard drive. Opening the file directory, he started copying everything he could, including all the personal files, pictures, videos, and whatever else he could find.

He looked out to see Vice Principal Winters get on the lawn mower in time to divert it from the prize-winning flowers. However, it was at the expense of the fence as he crashed through it, sending parts of the fence airborne. Simon's father and the woman he was kissing scrambled to get out of the hot tub. The night air was cool, and the woman wrapped a towel around her bikini-clad self to help keep herself warm. Simon's father noticed Michelangelo grabbing the camera and started yelling at him. The girl, now terrified at the events happening, grabbed the rest of her clothes, ran to her car, and drove off. Simon's father, Mr. Trendul, started chasing after Michelangelo, but lost him as Michelangelo exited the backyard. Vice Principal Winters shut off the lawn mower in time to see Mr. Trendul limping back into his backyard and the girl gone. Assuming it was a prank by one of the middle school students, Vice Principal Winters scanned his yard for some evidence of any other pranks.

After finished scanning for other pranks, Vice Principal Winters turned to Mr. Trendul and apologized, "I am sorry she ran off, but since it is late, I think we should wrap things up for now."

Mr. Trendul was about to respond when he glimpsed Cornelius and asked, "Who is that?"

Vice Principal Winters turned around to look at what Mr. Trendul asked about and saw nothing. He was about to dismiss Mr. Trendul's suspicion as paranoia after the prank, and stated, "You must excuse my students from time to time. They try to show how clever they are and pull a prank. However,…" Suddenly, he thought he glimpsed Cornelius at his computer, and moved in closer to verify.

Cornelius knew he was about to be spotted, but refused to stop his progression. Suddenly, Vice Principal Stevens confirmed what he saw, and started yelling at him. Cornelius ran to the back door and locked it within a fraction of a second before Vice Principal Winters could open it. Somehow, he dodged a direct line of sight of Vice Principal Winters, even though he knew it was Cornelius, and started yelling at him directly. Cornelius would not be deterred and chanced the extra trouble he would be in and returned to the computer to wait for the transfer to be complete.

Vice Principal Winters tried the back door for a second or two before disappearing from Cornelius' sight to try other ways into his house. Cornelius could hear him trying the other various ways and knew his time was running out. Suddenly, the computer chimed, and signaling the completion of file copying. He packed the external hard drive and the USB cable into his pockets as Simon's father broke the glass in the back door, granting them access to the house once again. Cornelius never intended to leave the way he came in, and before they could figure out what was happening, he already escaped through the front door. He ran as fast as he could to where they had stashed their bikes. Smiling as he saw Michelangelo waiting for him. They shook hands briefly, got on their bikes, and they were off to Cornelius' house. Determined to get there before anyone could realize they left or what they were up to.

As they approached the house, they slipped into the backyard and reentered the garage from the back door. They put the bikes back where they belonged and started looking for Cornelius' father's old computer, which he stored in a box somewhere in the garage. After they found it, they started setting it up, and upon completion, they turned it on. Thrilled as it came to life, and after it finished loading, they started going through the files. Suddenly, the lights to the garage came on and Grandpa Saul was looking down at them from the landing, connecting the house and the garage. "What is going on in here?"

"I think we have what we need to prove, John McCutty's innocence," Cornelius stated as he was pulling up different files.

"Where have you been?" asked Grandpa Saul as he wheeled down the ramp. Upon reaching the bottom of ramp he continued, "Do not bother telling me anything but the truth. I have been on the phone with Principal Stevens. He is furious and has determined there will be an expulsion hearing on Monday." He waited until they gave him the undivided attention and once they did, he continued, "Did you really break into Vice-Principal Winters' home? Did you think you would get away with it? Do you know if you gather evidence while breaking the law yourself, the court can deem it inadmissible and may not help John McCutty? Did you know, even if it is what we need to free John McCutty, the one responsible for the crime could go free? Do you realize you could have affected your futures by this incident forever?"

Grandpa Saul paused for a moment before continuing, "Now, it is late, and you should get back to bed. The both of you. We will try to gain control of this in the morning."

Cornelius unplugged the external hard drive before they retreated to the safety of his room.

# The Apology

The next morning, Cornelius woke up at his typical time, started his normal wake-up procedure, and when he turned to jump out of bed, he noticed Michelangelo still sleeping on the floor. He avoided interrupting Michelangelo's sleep by maneuvering around him to get access to the door. Once he reached the door, he silently exited his room. Taking care of what else he needed before he began his journey down the stairs, he noticed the things typical to Saturday morning, the birds chirping, spring fighting for its moment through the tail end of winter, and the sun rising. He took a deep breath as his foot set on the main floor of the house. A smile graced his face, for this was his usual favorite time of the week. It was during the still of Saturday morning. The house was his and his alone, at least until the others woke up. However, this Saturday morning he would have to share. He could hear Grandpa Saul's voice echoing softly in the house as he was talking to someone on the phone, and he did not look happy. Once they made eye contact, Grandpa motioned for Cornelius to come over and sit in a chair beside him. Cornelius complied and sat in the chair while listening to Grandpa Saul finish his conversation with several versions of, "I understand. Of course. We will be there."

Once he finished the phone call, he returned the phone to the base charger, took a deep breath, turned to Cornelius, and started, "That was Principal Stevens. We are to report Monday for a disciplinary hearing with pending expulsion." He took another deep breath to keep calm before continuing, "You have got in over your head. Furthermore, I do not see how this is going to break and bend in your favor." He paused for several seconds, which felt like hours, to Cornelius, before continuing, "However, we will try. We have two days to fix this and hopefully stop this from becoming an avalanche." Grandpa Saul paused for several moments as he pulled a notebook out of his pocket and started leafing through it. Finding what he was looking for, he picked up the phone handset and continued, "I need to make several calls. Go on about your business, and please, stay out of trouble."

Cornelius nodded in compliance as he got up from the chair and started his morning routine. About halfway through his cereal,

Michelangelo came down and sat across from him. Cornelius got up, got a glass, bowl, and spoon, and placed them in front of Michelangelo. He slid him the cereal before going to the fridge to retrieve the milk and orange juice to place them in front of Michelangelo.

Michelangelo poured himself a glass of juice, drank the entire thing, and poured another while prepping his cereal. After a couple of mouthfuls of cereal, Michelangelo asked, "What do we do next?"

"There is a lot we have to accomplish, especially if we want to get it done before your mother comes home. However, the first thing we need to do is make two copies of the external hard drive onto flash drives and get Grandpa Saul up to speed."

Michelangelo finished his bowl of cereal and poured himself another. As he took a couple of mouthfuls, he asked, "Then what?"

"We do what I hope is one of our strongest moves," Cornelius replied.

"What is that?" asked Michelangelo.

"Make it up as we go," replied Cornelius.

Once they finished eating, Cornelius and Michelangelo made copies of the external hard drive onto the flash drives and added a copy of the video they got from Vice Principal Winters' home to each. They then deleted the video they made from the camera. Cornelius stated one of the flash drives was for them, one for Plan B, and the external hard drive was for Grandpa Saul. Upon finishing, they waited for Grandpa Saul to finish the call he was on and got him up to speed on everything they found. Grandpa Saul took a break from the information they gave him, looked up at them, and stated, "This is good information. However, how you got it is questionable. I have a lot more phone calls to make, and I need you two to stay out of trouble while I do. Can you do that?"

"There is a high probability," replied Cornelius.

Michelangelo answered, "Yes!"

"Do you think we can pull this off?" Cornelius asked.

"We will need one hell of a Hail Mary, some faith, and a lot of favors," replied Grandpa Saul as he motioned for the two of them to move along and dialed his first call.

Cornelius made his way to the garage directly, with Michelangelo in tow. Once they got in, they got the bikes off the bike rack, grabbed their helmets, Michelangelo grabbed Cornelius' arm and asked, "What is the plan?"

"Every weekend, Simon and his dad go somewhere for the weekend. It is one of the major reasons we can enjoy our weekends," responded Cornelius.

"What does that have to do with what is going on?" asked Michelangelo.

"We need to go at this from a different angle. Follow me," answered Cornelius.

They rode through the streets discreetly until they got in position to see Simon's house. Pulling their bikes behind some bushes, they waited as Simon and his dad finished packing their car and left. Cornelius stood up as their car turned the corner and disappeared. As Michelangelo stood up, Cornelius tapped him on the shoulder and stated, "I need you to head back to the house."

"Why?" asked Michelangelo.

"Because most of what is happening is my fault. It is bad enough we are facing expulsion on Monday, but if this goes bad. I need you, as my friend, to be far away from it," he stated.

Michelangelo reluctantly agreed, and as he rode off, Cornelius started walking toward Simon's house.

Simon's house was one of the three biggest on the street and one of the seven biggest in town. It screamed old money and was imposing in its design. However, determined to carry out the next part of Plan B, Cornelius opened the gate, closed it behind him, and continued toward the door. The yard was immaculate, not a blade of grass out of place nor a stray leaf lying about. The front porch wrapped around the house with an ornate railing, and the stairs up to the porch fanned out, allowing a great place for staged pictures. Walking up to the door, he took a deep breath before ringing the bell, and waited for Mrs. Trendul, aka. Simon's mom, to answer. He knew she was home, because he saw her kiss her husband and son goodbye before they left. Four or five horrible minutes went by, until the door opened, and Mrs. Trendul asked, "Did you forget something?" She did a double take, realized it was not her family, tightened the robe she was wearing and continued, "I know you. Aren't you the child that Simon had trouble with before spring break? Yes, you almost got Simon expelled!" She paused a second before she started closing the door.

Cornelius cleared his throat as his words hesitated for a second before continuing, "I am sorry for bothering you. However, I was wondering if I could have a moment of your time?"

"Why should I bother?" she asked as the door continued to close slower.

"I would like to clarify a few things," Cornelius started as the door closed. He paused as it latched shut, and then shouted, "I fear I owe you the sincerest of apologies and I would like to do so in person!"

The door unlatched and opened enough to peek out, and she stated, "Keep your voice down. The neighbors do not need to know my business." She paused for a second as she debated if she wanted to close the door, but before she did she asked, "For what you and Simon have gotten in to?"

Cornelius flashed a smile before continuing, "The relationship between Simon, myself, and countless classmates is what I would like to clarify. However, I need to apologize for what is about to happen."

She hesitated for a few seconds before opening the door fully, and asked, "Will you come in?" Cornelius stepped into her house. She escorted him to the sitting room, she motioned for him to take a seat, he sat down, and she continued, "It is not appropriate for me to entertain without being properly dressed. I will be right back." She left the room and went upstairs. Several moments later, she came back downstairs, with a very elegant blue dress with a matching jacket on, and sat across from Cornelius and stated, "Please continue."

"To begin, you must know, my intentions were to help. Not to cause any of the events about to unravel," Cornelius stated.

"What is about to unravel?" she asked.

"To clarify, I believe Simon's father has influenced Simon's actions to almost a core level. He is at a turning point and from this moment forward, he has only two paths he can go down. First, the path of one who pushes and punches his way through life. Second, he can correct it and gain control of it, to his and society's benefit. You must assert your influence, or he will end up like his father."

"And you think ending up like his father is a bad thing?" Mrs. Trendul asked.

He paused for a second before continuing, "You and I know it is!"

She flashed a smile in response.

Cornelius continued, "Mr. Trendul is one of the best contractors in the community, and known for his generous donations throughout the city. However, what is far less known is the significant achievements you have done, or because of your actions allowed someone else's achievements to shine. You have been secretly a beacon of hope, influence, and guidance to many people in this town through your countless organizations, charities, and businesses. I thank you on behalf of the entire town."

Her face was a little flush as she asked, "How could you possibly know any of this?"

"I listen, observe, and come to conclusions. Much like Sir Arthur Conan Doyle said through Sherlock Holmes, 'Once you eliminate the impossible, whatever remains, no matter how improbable, must be the truth.' I did the math, eliminated the impossible, and concluded your husband could not be the generous benefactor of our town." He paused for a second as he looked at her before continuing, "After further investigation, I ruled out the obvious and the impossible until the connections of this unknown benefactor started forming. In the end, the only conclusion was you. Again, thank you for all you do."

She smiled at the compliment and asked him to continue.

"You should take the credit and let the town know how great you are," he interjected before continuing. "This is why I must apologize." Pausing for a moment to gather his thoughts before continuing, "I was following a case to help John Saul McCutty and did not know the extent of what I got into until I was in over my head. For what is about to happen, I will take the responsibilities and the consequences of my actions. In the end, I and the people who helped me are just children, and I fear adults will not take us seriously. What I found during my investigation will affect you and how it does will depend on how ready you are for it when it comes out."

Taking the conversation seriously, she asked, "And what is about to be unveiled?"

"I am not sure," he replied.

"Then why are we here?" she asked.

Cornelius reached in his pocket and pulled out one of the flash drives. He set it on the coffee table between them, holding it in place with his finger, and continued, "We got the evidence we needed to free John Saul McCutty from Vice Principal Winters' home computer. However, we found much more evidence of other things that need to be stopped. Also, other things happening or about to, and information I believe you can help with." He lifted his finger and released the flash drive before continuing, "Help us or not, this is your choice, and we will respect it. However, this evidence is already in motion and will come out. There are several videos retrieved from Vice Principal Winters' computer. I thought you should be able to see what they were before they become known to the public and respond to it in the way you want to."

He got up and to walk out, and stopped as she asked, "What is on the flash drive?"

"I am not one hundred percent sure since I did not look at the videos. We read the doctored files, found the originals, and traced the money. My colleague and I made a video when we were there. We kept the files, but I copied the video we made and the videos on Vice Principal Winters' computer onto this flash drive for you to have. I gave a copy of all the other files to Grandpa Saul and the other adults involved. No one has seen what is on the videos, myself included, and they will not, unless you choose to let them." He paused as he opened the door and added before leaving, "You do so much for so many. You deserve the recognition. I know the ones you help would love to appreciate the one who is truly responsible, so they can show you their appreciation. With your demeanor, it would not be bad to bask in the light of your accomplishments from time to time, rather than linger in the dark. Again, for what is about to happen, I apologize." He smiled and left her house.

Michelangelo rode back to Cornelius' house. As he pulled into the garage, Cleopatra startled him by asking, "Hello, and where is my brother?" He was shy around girls and replied with a smile. Smiling back, she waited for a response before continuing, "I know the two of you went somewhere, and yet, here you are without him."

"He sent me back," replied Michelangelo.

She came down the stairs, and asked, "Is he alright?"

"Yes, he went to talk to Mrs. Trendul," Michelangelo responded. As she was about to speak, Michelangelo continued, "Can I ask you some questions?"

"About Cornelius?" she asked.

"Yes," he replied suspiciously.

"I figured it was about time you needed an outside opinion about Cornelius," replied Cleopatra. She took a breath, as she walked over to the desk, looked at it admiringly, and continued, "My name is Cleopatra Shelly Montegue. You can call me Cleo. Do you want me to barrel through a lot of information for you, or did you need this to be more a question-and-answer kind of thing?"

"How about we mix it up?" replied Michelangelo.

"Okay, mix it up, it is," she replied as she sat on top of one of many odd chests in the garage. Their parents liked to put things in waterproof chests to protect the various things they found on their many adventures. "So, by this point, I am sure you have realized he is unique?"

"That is one way to put it," Michelangelo retorted.

She smiled before asking, "It has happened to you, hasn't it?"

"What has happened?" replied Michelangelo, as he looked away from her for a moment.

"Ahh, Ahh, Ahh. It has happened to you! So, when was it?" Cleopatra asked optimistically.

"I am still not sure what you are talking about?" Michelangelo replied while trying to dodge the question.

"You know, the moment when you realized he is more complicated than he lets on," she started. She stopped to look at him intensely before continuing, "No! You had thee moment, the moment when you realize he is something greater than you thought!"

"Okay," he shouted. "Yes! Are you happy?"

"More than you can imagine, please continue," she said excitedly while inching to the edge of the chest she was on.

"Fine, it was the day we got suspended from school," started Michelangelo. "Simon had just slammed the door of Erin's locker onto her hand. She screamed out in pain, and Simon started yelling at her. Suddenly Cornelius charged Simon. They slammed into the lockers together, and they rolled to the ground. Cornelius forced the roll to go his way and somehow slammed Simon into a locker. It looked as if he tried to pass it off as a clumsy attempt to gain distance from Simon. However, when he sprang to his feet free of Simon, it proved otherwise, although when he got to his feet Simon to tackle him into the lockers on the other side of the hallway. Suddenly, Simon started pounding on your brother until your brother fell to the ground. This did not stop Simon as he started kicking him. Erin jumped on Simon's back and started hitting him. Simon stopped kicking your brother and threw her into the lockers. Your brother got back up and called him out. Simon knocked him down. However, he got back up, calling him out again as he stood up. This happened four more times, and each time Cornelius got up slower than the time before. Finally, the last time your brother stood up, Simon wound up a large punch and was about to hit him in the face." Michelangelo paused for a moment as he smiled and recalled the moment, before continuing, "Your brother would not back down, but he was about to get seriously hurt. I could not stand there anymore. So, I stepped in between them, caught Simon's punch, and that is when Principal Stevens stepped in."

"Yeah, that was the moment," replied Cleopatra. She smiled before asking, "Then what happened?"

"We were all in front of Principal Stevens. He asked us what happened. Cornelius was absolutely unbelievable, which is why we all probably got suspended, anyway."

"Let me guess, he somehow took full responsibility while making everyone else look as if they were trying to help him."

"Exactly! He stated he fell down the stairs. Simon and Erin saw this travesty of gravity and came to his aid to stop the vicious assault of the stairs. However, the stairs were not an opponent to be reckoned with, as in the end, they all got wrapped together and rolled down them, anyway. Until they bounced into me, wrapped me up with them before coming to a complete stop as we slammed into the lockers. He then spun it to stated that I supposedly was helping them up, when Principal Stevens showed up on the scene." Michelangelo paused before continuing, "Principal Stevens did not buy it for a second. Assured us the nearest staircase was at the other end of the very long hall they were in and demanded the true story. Cornelius never wavered from his story and the harder Principal Stevens pressed him for information, the better and more precise his story became. In the end, Principal Stevens stated that the security camera in the hall picked up the entire fight. Cornelius looked at him almost crossly, and stated, 'I would not trust what you see on the camera. With the correct equipment and dedicated person, the video could be altered.'" Michelangelo paused as he finished the story, before asking Cleopatra, "Now, can I ask you a question?"

"First, I never heard the complete story. All I can say is wow!" She paused as she got off the chest and started pacing while mumbling to herself.

Michelangelo gave her a few seconds before interrupting by asking, "Now, for my question? Is there something inherently wrong with Cornelius? I mean, does he have a condition I should know about, or is it something else?"

She stopped in mid-stride, turned on her heel to face him, and replied, "Of course not! He does not think like you or me. He is complex."

"I know, the Complicated Corkboard thing, right?" Michelangelo interrupted.

She chuckled for a second before replying, "The Corkboard of Complex Coincidences. He does not like it when you get the names wrong, especially his name."

"Yeah, he corrected me more than once," replied Michelangelo, with a hint of laughter in his voice.

"He gathers information like they are pieces of a giant jigsaw puzzle. However, it is a patient and lengthy process which he is constantly updating until the pieces form a picture. Once that picture comes into place, he uses 'The Corkboard of Complex Coincidences' to organize the data as it focuses. Before it, he would get lost in the shuffle of all the information. As far as his actions go, he looks at life as if it was a giant chess game. Each piece has a job to do, and it is his job to decipher or decide how each chess piece is best used. This is the best way I know how to explain it."

"So, he is human?" asked Michelangelo.

"Not that he would ever admit it," Cleopatra replied.

They laughed together for a few seconds, until Michelangelo asked, "All kidding aside, how smart is he?"

She walked over to his desk, pointed out the garage door to point out Cornelius was on his way back, and pulled out a small notebook and pen from his desk. She ripped out a piece of paper from the notebook, wrote something on it (on a surface no one could copy what she wrote), and folded the paper in half while handing it to Michelangelo. She looked at Michelangelo while putting the notebook and pen back and stated, "Ask him the same question and then compare it to my note."

As Cornelius rode into the garage, he got off his bike, put it away, and asked what they were talking about. Cleopatra got back up on the waterproof chest and stated, "Just how you look at the world as a giant chessboard."

He smiled as he walked over to his desk, opened the drawer she had opened, and rearranged the notebook and pen back into their appropriate place. Looking at them both before responding, "You are both correct and incorrect at the same time. I do not view the world as one giant chess board. Rather, that you are playing a separate game of chess with each person or situation demanding such attention."

"Now that you are here, I wanted to talk to you," stated Cleopatra as she stood up and got as serious as she knew how to do.

"Of course," replied Cornelius. However, before she could speak again, he continued, "If it is regarding the end of 'The Detective Big Hat Agency', I understand."

"You do," she replied with surprise in her voice.

Cornelius stopped and stared at her with an unending commitment in sight, which again felt like an eternity to Cornelius and an awkward two minutes for both Cleopatra and Michelangelo. However, just as they thought Cornelius was in his reboot state, he continued, "The writing has been on the wall for the last couple of years and now that I am getting older, it seems appropriate. I will continue my investigations though, with the help of my new partner, since you would like to step away from this."

"Are you sure this is alright with you?" Cleopatra asked.

"Absolutely," Cornelius replied as Cleopatra hugged him.

"I am so glad you understand, but I will be there for you when you need me," Cleopatra stated as she released the hug and straightened his shirt.

Michelangelo cleared his throat and, once their attention was on him, he asked, "I am not sure what this is about, but I have two questions.

First, Cleo has given this paper and told to ask you a question." Cleopatra turned to face Michelangelo with a smile brightening her face.

Cornelius turned to make eye contact and asked, "What is your question?"

"This is going to sound weird this way," Michelangelo started. Took a deep breath, and continued, "Just how smart are you, exactly?"

Cornelius flashed a smirk across his face and asked, "And your second question?"

"Now, with Detective Big Hat Agency closing, where do we go from here?"

Cornelius walked over to his desk and removed the sign on a piece of laminated paper on the side of his desk that said, 'Detective Big Hat Agency.' He put in the bottom of his tiered filing system.

"First, intelligence is hard to gauge. Some people own it, while other shy away from it, and the majority flop around in the middle. In the end, I hope I am as smart as I need to be at the moment I need to be." Cleopatra giggled for a second while pointing at the piece of paper she gave Michelangelo. Michelangelo opened, and it repeated word for word what Cornelius had just stated. Quickly closing the paper, he got from Cleopatra in time to watch him open a drawer in the desk and pulled out a personalized name plate for his desk, which said,

### Cornelius Montegue
### Unlicensed Private Junior Investigator

Cleopatra gave Cornelius a quick kiss on the cheek and was about to head into the house when she noticed Grandpa Saul on the platform connecting the house to the ramp. Commanding respect without a single word, he waited as he got their attention one by one, and once he did, he started down the ramp. Keeping as much eye contact as he could as he rolled down the ramp onto the garage floor. Silence consumed the garage as he rolled over to them. He looked at Cornelius and asked, "Where have you been?"

"I have been running down the field for a Hail Mary of my own," Cornelius stated as he looked at the floor. He took a deep breath before looking up at Grandpa Saul with a smirk of disappointment, and continued, "Or at least started some of my own damage control."

Grandpa Saul smiled in approval, before stating, "I have been working hard at getting ahead of this situation as well. That is why I asked Officer Winston Butusov to come over and review everything the two of you have gathered to see if we can save your academic career. That is why we are going to join Officer Butusov in the kitchen, so we can go over the finer points."

As they walked into the house, Cornelius made sure he held back with Michelangelo until they were the last ones in the garage. Just before they went into the house, Cornelius stopped him and stated, "I should not have assumed, therefore, I shall ask instead. Would you like you to join my new agency? You would be a most valuable partner."

Michelangelo smiled, and responded, "Of Course!" They shook on it and went into the kitchen.

For the next couple of hours, they went over their case. However, Officer Butusov agreed with Grandpa Saul about the weakness of the case. As he was about to leave, he turned to Cornelius and stated with a tone of concern, "You did solid work."

"Thanks," responded Cornelius questionably.

Officer Butusov continued, "Hang on a second. In the past you have done well as Detective Big Hat, however, you were not taking on bigger tasks. You did solid work, but not good work. You broke the rules to gain what you needed by any means, which makes you about as good as those you are opposing. What is worse, you have not gained any concrete evidence of any kind to lock down the case. Concrete Evidence such as, Hard Undeniable Evidence, a Confession, Witness to the Crime, Video Evidence, or Caught them in the Act. What you have is a hunch, motive, and enough pieces of the puzzle to string together a case that a talented attorney will destroy in court. Now, with your expulsion on the line, we have less than forty-eight hours to fill in the pieces, or the fallout could be more than you can handle." Cornelius stared at him as he spoke. Then Officer Butusov paused for a second, came in close to Cornelius, and continued, "As Detective Big Hat, you have proven you are brilliant, cunning, and persistent in your drive for discovering the truth. However, it is not enough to be smarter than the people you are investigating. To be the best, you must be better, and more importantly, precise. You have extraordinary compassion and drive, but you need an ironclad case without holes to be ripped apart by a talented attorney. Also, to prevent yourself from falling into a trap of those you oppose, no matter what you do, you must be several steps ahead of your opponent. The more sinister the Criminal the more you have to get ahead of their plans, or the repercussions could echo for years to come."

"I understand," replied Cornelius.

"I look forward to your future exploits and who knows if we will end up working together again someday," finished Officer Butusov before leaving for the night.

The rest of the day was uneventful as they tried to distract themselves from the approaching storm.

# To Be Suspended, or Not To Be

Sunday was an uneventful day as they did their best to prepare for the Expulsion Hearing on Monday. Michelangelo's mom came to pick up him around noon and she talked to Grandpa Saul about the Expulsion Hearing for an hour or two. At first, she did not want Michelangelo hanging out with Cornelius again, however, after she and Grandpa Saul talked, she realized the influence Cornelius was having on him. Michelangelo's grades were going up, and she had gotten more than a few calls from parents of other classmates about how Michelangelo and Cornelius have been a positive influence around the school. In the end, she agreed they would take on the Expulsion Hearing together and fight it as best as they could. After she left, Grandpa Saul, Cleopatra, and Cornelius avoided each other when they could and went on with their daily business until it was time for bed.

The next morning, Cornelius woke up and went through his normal routine. He got ready for school and as soon as he went for the door to leave, Grandpa Saul stopped him and stated, "You can ride in with us." He paused as he looked at Cleopatra and continued, "Run along and do not be late for school."

"Good luck," Cleopatra added as she gave a kiss on the cheek to Cornelius.

After the sneak attack peck on the cheek, Cornelius turned to Grandpa Saul and asked, "Us?"

"Yes, we are going in with the McCutty's. Officer Butusov instructed us to all be present for the Expulsion Hearing. Michelangelo and his mother will join us there."

Shortly after, the McCutty's pulled up in a van that was retrofitted for a wheelchair, honking as they pulled up to the curb. Grandpa Saul and Cornelius exited through the garage, punched in the code to close the door behind them, and got into McCutty's van. Old McCutty had his old van converted when he found out Grandpa Saul was moving in with us and has become his personal transport, never missing a single time Grandpa Saul needed transported.

A few moments later, they arrived at the school, and Grandpa Saul was unloaded. They took a deep breath and the four of them went into the school. The town's only two detectives used a special car given to them by the county, two police cars and another one were in the spots immediately next to Old McCutty's van. Cornelius pointed out they were there as they walked into the building. John McCutty's nerves were getting the best of him, and his hand started twitching. Old McCutty could not help but to notice his son's agitation and stopped as they got in the building, and stated, "Relax, we have a good chance of getting your name cleared today."

John stopped and turned to face the three of them and responded, "At what expense? The ones who found the proof might get expelled, and the ones who framed me will probably get away."

"Framed you," a booming voice called out from around the corner and down the hall. They walked around the corner and saw both Simon and Simon's dad, both in expensive suits, and both standing proud as peacocks. Once they got in eyesight of Simon's dad, he continued, "Framed is such an ugly word. I am sure this is a giant misunderstanding and once they expel both Cornelius and Michelangelo. We can clear this matter up." He launched his commercial cheesy smile as if he held all the power in this situation.

Michelangelo's mother smiled as she asked, "We are in this until it completely plays out. Right, Saul?"

"Correct Dianna," responded Grandpa Saul.

The hallway was suddenly as silent as it has ever been, until Michelangelo broke the silence and stated, "Your first name, no one is allowed to use your first name."

She smiled at her son, gave him a quick shake of the chin, and stated, "Only my friends can."

Before the conversation got any deeper, Receptionist Tami opened the door to the outer office and asked them all to come in. There were enough chairs for everyone. However, with the added wheelchair of Grandpa Saul, it was a little more crowded than it should be. Cornelius noticed two files on Receptionist Tami's desk, the smaller file of Michelangelo Durelly, and a file about five times larger file of his. Once everyone found a seat, she used her phone to call into Principal Stevens' office, where all the shouting was coming from. Principal Stevens hushed everybody as he picked up the phone. Receptionist Tami informed Principal Stevens about Simon, Michelangelo, Cornelius, their appropriate parents, and the McCutty's. After she hung up the phone, she made her apologies to the adults, grabbed the files, and went into Principal Stevens' office. Cornelius noticed this was the second time he saw her get up from her desk. After she entered the office, you could hear him giving instructions to her, but Cornelius could not make them out. After Principal Stevens finished, she came back into the outer office and asked Grandpa Saul, Mrs. Durelly, and Mr. Trendul to follow her through the adjoining door to the conference room. Leaving the McCutty's in the outer office with Cornelius, Michelangelo, and Simon. They went into the conference room, a couple of minutes later, Receptionist Tami exited, and stated to the ones she left in the room, "Let me know if I can get anyone a water or anything."

Cornelius got a glimpse into the much bigger conference room, and he could see a table set up with enough chairs for the adults involved. The doors closed and Michelangelo nudged Cornelius to look at Simon, who was both smiling about his new suit and their fate. A few seconds later, the discussion stopped in Principal Stevens' office, the door opened, and Vice Principal Winters stormed out, heading straight toward Cornelius and Michelangelo. However, Principal Stevens stopped him by stating his name in a disciplinary tone, and Vice Principal Winters loomed over the pair of them for a moment before storming into the teacher's lounge. One of the town's detectives, followed by Officer Butusov, or Officer Buttons as Grandpa Saul calls him, exited the office, and went into the conference room. Finally followed by Principal Stevens, who instructed Receptionist Tami to watch the three of them until they were ready to talk to them.

The office was situated so they could see the parking lot and they had a good view of Old McCutty's van. As time passed, the silence was deafening except for the occasional outburst from the conference room. Until Cornelius asked, "If you do not mind me asking, why are the two of you here, Mr. McCutty?"

"Officer Butusov asked us to be here," replied Old McCutty. He could see Cornelius was about to follow up, and cut him off, "No, I do not know why."

Nothing else was said, for the next half an hour, and time appeared to slow to a stop, when suddenly Cornelius' interest was captured and intrigued by the three high-class cars pulling up to the building. He nudged Michelangelo to point it out. Unfortunately, before he could find out any more information, Receptionist Tami's desk phone started ringing. She answered it and told Cornelius, Michelangelo, and Simon they could go in. Simon cut Cornelius and Michelangelo off from the conference room entrance, and they let him go through first rather than argue. As they entered the conference room, Principal Stevens motioned for them to sit in the three chairs open in the middle of the table.

Once they sat down, Principal Stevens started, "This is a very unusual case. We have brought the three of you here to discuss your expulsions."

"Three of us! What did I do?" interrupted Simon.

"You were on warning. Your attitude, general lack of respect to your teachers and myself during the Science Fair, and your suspected interference in Erin Walker's project is more than enough for me to send you home for the rest of the year."

Simon went to retort however, his father interrupted with both a diplomatic and commanding tone, "Simon." Simon silenced himself instantly.

Principal Stevens smiled before continuing, "As for the two of you? There is a charge of breaking and entering filed by Vice Principal Winters, both to his office and his home."

"I was the only one involved in these supposed claims," Cornelius interrupted.

"Noted," Principal Stevens stated as he made a note. "We have come up with a punishment that fits all involved. However, before we move on to the punishment. Detective Harper needs a moment."

Detective Harper stood up and replied, "Thank you."

Suddenly, there was a knock on the door to the outer office and Principal Stevens excused the interruption and went to open the door. He opened the door and stepped out for a moment. After a few seconds, he came back into the conference room, cleared his throat and stated, "I am sorry we have to pause these proceedings for a moment. I will return in a moment." Detective Harper sat down again and waited for the return of Principal Stevens.

Silence filled the conference room during the absence of Principal Stevens. Several moments later, the door to the outer office opened, and Principal Stevens stepped in, holding the door for Mrs. Trendul as she walked in. She was holding a couple of binders, carrying her purse, and dressed professionally as if she was on a mission accompanied by three lawyers, an Assistant District Attorney, Detective Briggs, and two uniformed officers, Attorney Sam Churn (John McCutty's attorney), the Superintendent of the School District, and the McCutty's. Assistant District Attorney Paul Greston's business suit was top of the line, and he carried a designer briefcase. However, the lawyers who accompanied Mrs. Trendul out dressed and outclassed him in almost every way. Detective Briggs walked in and stood next to Detective Harper, who was now standing to allow one of the new attendees his chair. Attorney Sam Churn, John McCutty's attorney, and the McCutty's took up positions against the wall. The Superintendent of the School District walked in and took the seat left by Detective Harper, Principal Stevens closed the door, and took his seat next to the Superintendent. The two uniformed officers took up positions behind Vice Principal Winters and Mr. Trendul.

Mrs. Trendul stated as she came into the room, "Please forgive my intrusion, but the Assistant District Attorney and I have a few things to clear up." She walked up to her husband, bent over so he could only hear what she had to say, and added, "Thank you for giving me the evidence I needed for the full power of our prenup to be enforced. You have nothing now." She stood up and walked over to where Principal Stevens was sitting. Glancing at the Assistant District Attorney as she handed him a blue binder she was carrying, and continued, "I have just handed the Assistant District Attorney, the full ledger of the transactions between my husband, Simon Maxwell Trendul II, and Vice Principal Winters. It details all the work my husband has done for the school and what they billed to school district."

Mr. Trendul stood up and shouted, "Stop, you can't do this!" The uniformed officer behind him put a hand on his shoulder and gently helped him find his seat.

She smiled before continuing, "I can, I am, and I will." She handed the green binder to the Assistant District Attorney, and added, "This is the ledger of what it actually cost, the payouts to Vice Principal Winters, and the overhead he charged the schools in an excess of twelve million dollars." She walked over to the Superintendent of the Schools, reached out her hand, and the Superintendent of the Schools took it. As they shook hands, she continued, "The Assistant District Attorney issued warrants to lock both of their accounts, so we can sort this horrible violation of trust and professionalism out. I will be happy to reimburse the schools for their loss, plus twenty-three percent interest for their troubles. Which should reinstate both the arts and sports programs back in the curriculum."

"Yes, it will and thank you," replied the Superintendent of the Schools.

Mrs. Trendul walked back to the head of the table, before continuing, "Assistant District Attorney, my lawyers, Attorney Sam Churn, have gone over the files and have enough evidence to exonerate John McCutty." She motioned for the Assistant District Attorney to speak.

"The District Attorney's Office and I would like to express my apologies and have dropped all charges against John McCutty," he stated he walked over to John McCutty and shook his hand.

Principal Stevens and the Superintendent got up, approached John McCutty, shook his hand in turn, and Principal Stevens added, "In addition, we apologize for any inconvenience to you or your reputation. We have issued your back pay, and we have added a bonus to your pay for the inconvenience. That is, if you will have us back?"

"Thank you," John McCutty responded. He took the check, looked at Principal Stevens, and responded, "O... O... Of course, when can I start?"

Principal Stevens answered, "Excellent. You can start back on Monday."

Mrs. Trendul walked around the table and waited for her turn to shake his hand. Once she was able, she took his hands with both of hers and continued, "I am truly sorry for what my family has put you through. So, if you would do me the honor..." Pausing as she turned to one of her attorneys, accepted the check they produced, and turned back to him to continue, "Of accepting this check as personal compensation from my family to yours."

John McCutty took the check, looked at it, and replied as he handed it back to Mrs. Trendul, "This is too much. I cannot accept this."

"Please, use it for your retirement, vacation, to take a trip, or buy something you have always wanted. This is the least I can do." He said nothing, but hugged her instead. She hugged him in return, smiled, and said, "Excellent." After the hug, she paused for a second, and helped herself to one of the bottled waters on the table. Taking a long enough drink to only allow her only another small drink later, she continued, "My lawyers have the original files, the flash drive given to me with the evidence we need, and the video proving my husband's infidelity. My lawyers have started the divorce proceedings, and I will testify against my husband and Vice Principal Winters." She motioned for the District Attorney to speak as she drank the rest of her water.

He stepped up and stated, "Simon Maxwell Trendul II and Steven Winters, I hereby place you under arrest. Officers, please read them their rights and escort them to the police station for processing." The uniformed officers did as they were instructed and took the men out of the building. The Assistant District Attorney, Attorney Sam Churn, and John McCutty left so they could discuss things, and both detectives left the room.

So, Officer Butusov, the Superintendent, Principal Winters, Mrs. Trendul, Mrs. Durelly, Grandpa Saul, and the three in trouble remained in the room. The Superintendent took over the conversation, and stated, "I have discussed with Principal Stevens the severity of this case. Your records in the school, the testimonies in your behalf, and your intention may have been honorable. However, your reckless abandonment of the rules and your almost criminal behavior have left me no choice to suspend the three of you for the rest of the week. Your teachers have already compiled a merciless amount of work for you to complete during the week and I believe two papers each. This is your final warning, and comes with a major condition, if any of the three of you put one toe out of place for the rest of the year, we will carry out the expulsion."

Simon decided this was unfair, stood up, and shouted, "This is…"

"Simon Maxwell Trendul III, if you do not silence yourself this very second. The punishment you will suffer shall be tenfold when I get you home," stated Mrs. Trendul in a commanding, steady, and unwavering tone.

He replied with immediate silence and sat back down in his chair.

The Superintendent paused as this played out and took a drink of water before continuing, "Simon, you can go wait in the outer office." She waited as he exited. Once he did, she looked at Cornelius for several seconds, before continuing, "Cornelius, you were going to be expelled. I want you to understand the severity of this. It could set you back and possibly ruin your chances for certain colleges or other future endeavors.

However, since the two of you assisted the school in reacquiring stolen funds, helped John McCutty get his job back, helped with miscellaneous janitorial duties around the school, helped with tutoring, and helped secure Erin Walker her grant for winning the Science Fair. We instead offer our appreciation and the former deal you already heard." The superintendent took another drink of water before continuing, "Thank you for what you have done. I am sorry. I meant we thank both of you for what you have done. Now, if you could wait in the outer office, there are a few things the adults need to discuss." Michelangelo and Cornelius got up, thanked her, and walked to the outer office door. Cornelius took a deep breath of relief as he opened the door to the outer office, and they left as quietly as possible.

As the doors to the conference room closed, the pair took seats opposite Simon. He stared at them with near hatred for nearly twenty minutes, until he finally cracked and broke the silence by stating, "You are lucky this broke your way!"

"Are they really?" asked Simon's mom from the doorway of the conference room. She stepped through as the rest of the adults passed by, before continuing, "I found your ledger, too. Principal Stevens, may I use your office for a few minutes?"

"Absolutely," he responded as he went to the door, unlocked it, and motioned for them to go inside. As she closed the door, she added, "Cornelius and Michelangelo, could you wait in the hall with Mr. Montegue and Mrs. Durelly?" They nodded in acceptance as the doors closed, and before they could leave the outer office, you could hear her screaming at Simon Maxwell Trendul III.

Almost twenty minutes went by while the four of them waited outside in the hall. Finally, the door opened, and a defeated Simon shuffled out while keeping his eyes focused toward the floor. He walked up to Michelangelo and Cornelius and stated, "I am sorry for everything I have done, and from this moment forward I..." He paused as he looked back toward the outer office and saw his mother coming through the door. She gave him a look, pointed at him signaling him to continue, and he continued, "I will be a better student and friend to those around me."

Before he could say anything else, she snapped, "Now, go wait in the car!"

Simon left without hesitation, and she watched him all the way to the car. Once he was in the car, she turned to the four of them, smiled, and walked up to Mrs. Durelly. Cornelius could not help but notice she had a beautiful smile. She reached out her hand and as Mrs. Durelly shook it, she continued, "It is a pleasure to meet you, despite the circumstances. I hope someday we can be friends." Turning to Cornelius and Michelangelo, she continued, "Is this a hobby of yours, or do you like to interfere where you do not belong?"

Cornelius pulled a homemade business card he crafted out of a card holder he got from his father and always carried with him, which read:

### Cornelius Montegue
### Unlicensed Junior Private Detective

He paused as she read it, and added, "I hope my partner and I can make a living of this someday."

She smiled before responding, "Excellent, I trust you will know what to do with this." She handed him Simon's ledger and continued, "I will reimburse all the victims in this ledger, and I would like you to execute this task for me, under the watch of your grandfather, of course." She walked over to Grandpa Saul and handed him an envelope of cash, thanked him, and added before leaving, "Let me know if you need any more." However, instead of leaving, she stared at Cornelius and eventually asked, "You said you had copies of the videos?"

"Yes," replied Cornelius.

"And no one else has seen them?" she asked.

"Of course not. I have kept them safeguarded," Cornelius replied.

"Can I have them?"

"Absolutely, however, if you could make the arrangements with Grandpa Saul," he replied.

She took a deep breath of relief before continuing, "Thank you."

"You are most welcome," added Cornelius.

She turned to leave, but stopped in mid-motion, before turning back to add, "You have a bright career ahead of you, Cornelius." She smiled as she calculated her thoughts before continuing, "You were right, by the way." she smiled at him, before asking, "Could I ask you for another favor?"

He looked at her with a calculating stony stare before responding, "That depends on the favor."

Smiling again before asking, "If possible, could you please not give up on my son?"

Cornelius flashed a smile before answering, "I never did."

"Thank you," she responded, before turning to walk away.

After a few steps, Grandpa Saul bellowed, "Excuse me?"

She stopped and turned around again, and asked, "Yes, how can I help?"

"For those not in the loop. What was he right about?" grumbled Grandpa Saul.

Smiling as she walked up to Grandpa Saul, she pulled out a business card and handed it to him. As he looked it over, she continued, "Let me know if he needs help with his academic future." She paused as she looked at Cornelius before continuing, "You were right. It is good to get recognition for the things you do. To help make a difference in the light and not from the shadows. Until next time we meet." She turned and walked away.

Michelangelo and his mother left immediately after they arranged for Cornelius and Michelangelo to do their suspension work together.

Grandpa Saul and Cornelius made their way out to Old McCutty's van where Officer Butusov was talking to the McCutty's. As they approached, he said his goodbyes and approached Cornelius. He knelt so he could look him in the eye, and stated, "Congratulations, you pulled it off." He stood up before continuing, "This time! Next time, be better, be smarter, and leave luck up to those who need it." Detective Butusov put his hand out, Cornelius grabbed it, they shook, and parted ways.

Grandpa Saul turned to Cornelius and said, "Let's go home." Grandpa Saul turned to Cornelius and said, "Let's go home." They loaded up into the McCutty's van and had the most excited and quiet ride home.

After they got to their home, both Mr. McCutty and John McCutty shook Cornelius' hand until the front screen door on their home slammed open. They all turned to see what was going on, however, before anyone could realize what was it was Cleopatra had sprinted from the house, and wrapped Cornelius in the biggest hug she had ever given anyone. While hugging Cornelius with all her might, she stated, "I just heard about the art class." She let him go, looked him in the eye, and as her eyes welled up from pride she added, "Thank you."

# The Return of the Parents

Cornelius broke the rest of the week up into three parts. First, the completion of their homework. Second, to the vast chore list Grandpa Saul and Mrs. Durelly had for each of them. Finally, calling all the children in the ledger and arranging for them to meet him on Saturday. It was a long week, but Saturday finally came around.

Cornelius got up and went through his normal morning routine. Michelangelo came over at the scheduled time, exactly one hour before the children in the neighborhood were to arrive. There was an arrangement with the children coming in to get their money, but it was going to take all day. It was a rather large ledger. About a half an hour before the first of Simon's victims were to arrive, Erin Walker showed up and entered the garage. Cornelius had set up a table where Michelangelo, Cleopatra, Grandpa Saul, and he could sit and go through the colossal task ahead of them. Erin waited in the garage patiently until Cornelius came out again,

Without hesitation Cornelius asked, "Erin, it is early. Why are you here?"

"I want to help," she replied with her hands crisscrossed behind her back while shifting from foot to foot. Cornelius looked at her with his penetrating stare until she continued, "Where are you sitting?"

Snapping out of his trance, he responded, "Over there, the first chair as you come in the garage."

"That is a delightful spot. Do You have another chair?" she asked.

"Absolutely," Cornelius replied, with a quizzical look on his face. He came down the ramp, found an extra chair and handed it to her.

She took it, moved all the chairs down one spot, so her chair would be first, and when she finished, she stated, "There, now I will be seated next to you."

"I am not sure what is going on," he replied.

"I told you. I want to help," she replied with a smile.

"Alright then," he replied as he turned to go back into the house. Stopping before he went in the door, he asked, "Do you want some cocoa?"

"With marshmallows?" she asked, while making sure the seats were spaced adequately.

"Sorry, but we have whipped cream," he answered, still confused.

"Even better," she replied as she sat in her seat.

A few minutes later, he reentered the garage with cocoa for both. Michelangelo was following and held the door for both Cleopatra and Grandpa Saul. He was carrying his own Cocoa while Cleopatra was carrying both hers and Grandpa Saul's. Cornelius noticed a line was already forming as he placed Erin's cocoa in front of her.

Cornelius sat down next to her, then Michelangelo, Cleopatra, and finally Grandpa Saul. Grandpa Saul was carrying the cash box with the money to pay them back, and once he got into place, he started setting up as the cashier. Cornelius was to greet them and introduce the agency, Michelangelo was to help with the introductions and check their names off the list, Cleopatra was to write the receipts, and Grandpa Saul would count out the money.

As they were setting up, Erin leaned over to Cornelius, who leaned toward her in return, and she whispered, "By the way, I thought you would like to know that you are my boyfriend."

"Intriguing, do I get a say in this?" he whispered back.

"No, you will just over think it," she replied before giving him a kiss on the cheek and holding his hand until it was time for him to shake hands with the growing line of kids. Once everyone settled into their positions, Cornelius motioned for the first kid to walk up, and they started the refunds. Cornelius and Michelangelo apologized to everyone, clarified who they were, and verified how much the ledger said Simon owed them. Grandpa Saul counted the money, Cleopatra wrote the receipts and double checked the money before sending them on their way. Anyone that was owed over fifty Cornelius arranged for their parents to accompany them. Mrs. Trendul's attorneys took care of the three victims, owed over a hundred.

About halfway through the list, a taxi pulled up, the driver got out and started unloading the bags. The passenger door opened, and Cornelius and Cleopatra's parents stepped out of the taxi. They had never seen this many children at their home before and stopped in their tracks as their curiosity began to give them options. After a few seconds, they grabbed their luggage and made their way into the garage. Some children in the line helped them bring their bags into the garage. The children set the bags down where the Montegues directed and went back into their positions in the line. They looked around and were in wonderment of what was going on. Cornelius announced they would take a ten-minute break as they helped their parents with their things, and after the kid at the table received his refund, they greeted their parents.

Cleopatra hugged her mom, then her father, while stated she was glad they were home. Cornelius shook their hands while stating the same pleasantries before he and Michelangelo took their bags to their room. Erin came up and shook Mr. Montegue's hand before giving Mrs. Montegue a hug. When she finished, she stated she was Cornelius' girlfriend, and Cleopatra shrieked at the excitement of this, offered to get her parents a drink, and dragged Erin with her so they could talk.

Grandpa Saul stood fast guarding the money, and as the Cornelius, Michelangelo, Cleopatra, and Erin branched off to do their various errands before they started up again, the Montegue's came up and asked, "What is going on?"

However, before Grandpa Saul could reply, Cornelius came back out of the house and replied, "It is all under control, but we can explain, in detail, after we are done."

Mr. and Mrs. Montegue smiled, hugged, walked up the steps to go into the kitchen, and Mr. Montegue replied before they entered, "Looking forward to it, son."

———————⌢⌣———————

# The Following Morning

Jenna Arton was not sure when she closed the binder and set it on the floor. However, she noticed it on the floor neatly as her eyes cracked open from the grace of sunrise filling the morning sky. She smiled as she untangled herself from the chair she curled up in after she finished reading the story to Olivia. Her feet touched the cool floor of the hospital room, and they automatically started probing around for her boots. Upon finding them, she clumsily slipped her feet into them one at a time. After her feet settled into her hiking boots, she shifted in her chair so she could sit straight up, stood up, and stretched for a couple of seconds before she cracked her back. She rolled her shoulders, and they popped as they realigned, and her neck popped a few times as she shifted it back and forth. Once she was done, she took a deep breath to help her wake up, when the noises from the machines in the room finally registered in her waking mind, reminding her where she was.

She walked over to Olivia, sat down in the chair again, and grabbed her hand. Squeezing it enough to let her know she was here, and then kissing her hand before letting it go for the moment. She packed up her belongings in case she had to depart in a hurry. When suddenly, the sunrise erupted over the adjoining buildings, flooding the room with light, and disrupting her train of thought. She walked up to the window and stared out as her eyes started welling up. She convinced herself it was from the sudden influx of light. However, she shifted to crying softly and had to admit it was because of the state of her friend. Taking a deep breath before smiling and turning to Olivia. She looked at her still body, composed herself, and she said lovingly, "I know sunrises are your favorites. Please, come back so we can share them with you."

She was about to lose her composure when she heard the gentle but firm knock of Michelangelo tapping the glass separating Olivia's room and the outer room. Turning around, she saw Michelangelo smiling at her and holding up her favorite coffee. He motioned for her to join him, and she signaled him it would be just a minute. She walked over to Olivia and said, "I will be back as soon as I can. I know you will pull through." Pausing for a moment as she bent down to kiss her on the forehead. When she finished, she straightened Olivia's hair, looked at her longing, and said, "I love you." Turning to head out to Michelangelo, she stopped as she reached the door, turned back to her, and added, "Like an older sister. I don't want to make this weird."

As she exited the room, she stepped into the outer room and took her coffee from Michelangelo. She closed her eyes and took a deep breath of it. As the aroma barreled through her nose and into her lungs, she could feel herself waking up, and she took another deep breath before taking a long, soothing sip. Holding the coffee cup by her lips to enjoy the aroma as the taste and the warmth made its way into her stomach. She took another sip while keeping the coffee cup close to her nose. She smiled as the coffee reassured her of the reason for getting up in the morning. With the coffee cup still at her nose, she opened her eyes and looked at Michelangelo from behind the cup and asked, "What does he need me to do?"

———————————⌇———————————